Friends Don't Say Goodbye

Friends Don't Say Goodbye

By Caz May

Book 2 in The Always Only You Series

First Published 2019

ISBN 978-0-6484998-2-4

Published by Caz May

© Caz May 2018

To my bearded hero, my husband Cam.
Your love and support with this journey
means everything.

Table of Contents

Author's Preface

Hello lovely reader! I thank you for purchasing my book, your support means the world to this newbie author and i'm guessing or hoping you've read the first in this series,

'Roommates Don't Kiss & Tell'.

If you haven't then I suggest you read that first for this story to make a whole lot more sense and a lot more enjoyable to read. As this book is the second in the series it goes back to tell parts of story from book one in another characters point of view, as well as expanding on the new characters story that you don't find out about in book one.

Before we get into the story it's essential for you to take note of the following information. It will ensure you understand the story and enjoy reading it as much as I enjoyed writing it.

This story is set in my current city of Melbourne, Victoria, Australia. I've been a Melbourne girl for eleven years now and absolutely love the unique city life it offers. Some of the places in the story are fictional, and some are real.

At the end of the book you will find a slang glossary which contains most of the Australian slang references you will find in the story.

This story is told in first person alternating point of views. If there is only a chapter title then the chapter is told from the main protagonists' point of view. If another name is underneath the chapter title that chapter is narrated by another character.

Lastly, I leave you with some pronunciations for my characters names.

Austin/Aust: Aus-tin & Aus-t (main protagonist)

Kaden/Kad: Kay-den & K-ad-d

Annika/Anni: Ann-ic-a & An-e

Jairus/Jai: Jye-rus & Jye

I truly hope you enjoy the story.

Caz May

xx

Never say goodbye

because saying goodbye means going away

and going away means forgetting.

Peter Pan

Prologue | Dress in White

August 2018

It's absolutely freezing as I walk down Bridge Road, wearing only a tank top and trackies from leaving boxing. It has been such a sunny day, but as the sun is setting the cold is setting in quick.

Nearly at my ute, I'm about to unlock it when I see her.

Annika is struggling to carry a rather large suit bag towards a car parked just down from mine.

My heart pounds in my chest seeing her again, as we've not spoken since she left to live with Jairus and we'd had a major fight. She looks absolutely stunning, having cut her hair a little shorter it frames her heart shaped face.

Rain is starting to pelt down, making her run awkwardly with the suit bag until she bumps straight into me. I could move, ignore her even but instead I ask, "Anni, is that you?"

She looks up, completely taken aback by my presence.

"Hi Austin," she replies, shaking her head as though she can't believe I'm actually standing in front of her.

I don't say 'hi' back, instead state, "So Bella wasn't lying then?"

"No Aust, I'm marrying Jairus in December and I'm sorry I didn't tell you."

Her words stab at my still broken heart and I speak with malice in my tone, "Yeah, you could have told me Annika. I...I..."

"I thought you'd not want to know," she says in an apologetic tone.

"How can you say that Annika?" I ask not waiting for her response when I continue, "You were my best friend. I still love you and the fact you're going to be wearing that white dress whilst you marry someone else really hurts...more than you'll ever know."

"I'm sorry Austin, I really am," she protests in the sweet innocent way that always makes my heart ache.

"Yeah so am I Annika," I spit at her a little meaner in tone than I feel, "but I hope you're happy."

Smiling wide at me she replies, "I am Aust...I really am but I gotta go. Take care."

She leans forward, closer to me, almost invading my personal space as though she's contemplating hugging me.

I'm anticipating her hug and thinking about kissing her cheek, but instead I just smile as she walks away unlocking her car.

Getting in my ute, I watch her as she puts the suit bag in the back seat of her BMW and my heart shatters all over again, just like the day she said goodbye when she moved out with Jairus.
I want her to be happy, but with me, not with him. It isn't that I hate the guy, he's good for her and it's clear her family loves him but I miss my best friend.

Reversing the ute out of the car park to drive home, my mind wanders, thinking of what I could do to be best friends with her again. It would hurt to be back in her life, and still be in love with her, but not being in her life at all hurts a hundred times more.

One I Pack it Up

Eight Months Earlier-January, 2018

I've barely spoken to Anni since our fight about her confessing to being in love with Jairus. Her words stabbed at my heart so bad, I'd snapped at her. Hurling words at her, that I just didn't mean, I felt like a complete tool.

Honestly I wanted to apologise, but every time I opened my mouth nothing would come out or she'd give me a bad case of dagger eyes that made me retreat like a wounded dingo.

The tension in our apartment is like something out of a horror movie, as we all tip toe around each other. Jairus has been sleeping in her room since New Years, and Bella has shifted in as my roomie. She's hardly ever home, which at times I kinda like but at the same time I like going to sleep thinking about her lying in the bed across from me.

I'm still in love with Anni, but thinking about the couple of times I'd fucked Bella always makes me hard.

When she's lying across from me I look over at her whilst I sneakily jack off.

Watching the rise and fall of her chest oddly excites me.

I sometimes feel as though she's hiding something from me, that maybe she has feelings for me but I keep my trap shut. I'd rather keep the casual sex arrangement we have going on than talk about feelings.

Feelings were the enemy in my mind, as I always found it difficult to face mine. Telling Anni that I just wanted to be fuck buddies when I'd fallen in love with her was the stupidest decision I'd made in a long time, maybe in forever.

She's now packing up her stuff to move out, kneeling on her overly full suitcase trying to zip it up. I'm not going to let her walk out the door, out of my life without trying to make amends with her.

Stopping in the door jamb of her room, I laugh, "Need some help babe?"

"No Austin I don't. Leave me alone!" she snaps, sighing as she finally gets the zipper shut.

I can't tear my eyes away from her lean legs in the smallest denim shorts in existence.

Just that sight is enough to make my groin ache,

"Anni, please. Don't be like that," I beg.

"Like what Austin?"

"I don't know Anni...a bitch. I'm sorry ok."

"It's too late to be sorry Austin. You...you ruined us,"

she sighs, her words stabbing my heart.

"Anni, that's really harsh. I don't want to lose you."

"Yeah, well you should have thought about that

before you opened your mouth Austin."

The way she's deliberately using my full name is

vindictive, cruel and so not like her usual self.

"Are you sure about this Anni? Do you really love

him?"

She smiles, coming to stand next to me. My heart is

pounding in my chest, just hoping that maybe she's

finally going to forgive me.

"With all my heart Austin...I can't explain it," she

replies, her tone softer.

"Hmm, ok," I mutter walking out of her room, feeling

as though nothing has changed since our fight.

She's leaving in two days, but I already feel like she's

gone.

My heart is broken, shattered.

Love is supposed to be amazing, but for me so far it's

nothing but pain.

Two | Goodbye my friend

Anni comes running inside, after packing her final suitcases into Jairus' car.

Her hair is up so her ponytail is swishing from side to side. My mind wanders to the last time I was with her and I grabbed onto it whilst thrusting my cock into her hard.

Being with Bella is good, but it's nothing compared to how being with Anni had made me feel. I can't help but wonder if I'll ever get to feel that way again. Obviously, Anni has found something with Jairus that I can't give her and it makes me feel hollow, half a man.

Now I'm sitting on the couch, my thigh grazing against Bella's. Tears are stinging Anni's eyes as she steps up to the couch.

"I'm going to miss you guys," she sobs through her tears.

She appears taken aback when I stand up to hug her. A whimper escapes my lips as I pull her closer and tighter against my chest.

"Goodbye Anni, I'm sorry for everything," I whisper
to her, hoping that she'll maybe finally accept my
apology.

Even if she does, I'm not sure what I want from her,
as being friends would be painful whilst I'm still in
love with her.

Breaking free from my hug, she replies, "I'm sorry
too, Aust, can we still be friends?"

"I don't know. You broke my heart, and even though
I'm sorry I'm not sure," I reply before walking away.,
not able to look at her again. She watches me leave, I
can feel her eyes on my back and my heart feels like
it's shattering in my chest.

Flopping down on my bed I sigh, thinking back to the
last few years with Anni, wondering if just going
down the friends with benefits road was what ruined
us or if it was something else.

Her question of whether we could be friends again
flashes in my mind, as part of me wants nothing else
but the part that wins out is that I can't be in love
with her and be her friend.

Even getting involved with Bella hasn't made me love
Anni any less.

All I want to do is turn my feelings off, to not have to
feel anything. Anni hasn't even left and I'm already

missing her, missing the past memories we'd shared and wondering what our future could have been if Jairus had never responded to our advertisement.

It's my own fault, as I'd suggested a male roommate, thinking it would be better in a two bedroom apartment. I'd thought in some weird fucked up way that it was going to bring Anni and I closer, as i'd spend more time in her bed than in my own, but then Bella crashed into our house changing the dynamic all over again.

All I know is the Annika I love is walking out the door, moving on with her life, without me and my heart is completely shattered. Shattered in so many pieces I'm not sure I'll ever be able to put it back together.

I'm being a pansy, even I know that, but I've always been a tad sensitive when it actually comes to feelings.

Feelings and love, more importantly, weren't something I felt until now. I have to wonder if I'll ever feel the way I feel about Anni for someone else and if I even want to, as stupid as that is.

Closing my eyes, I drift to sleep singing to myself 'Goodbye my lover, goodbye my friend.'

In my mind I'm playing my guitar as I sing, making a mental note to get back into playing and writing some songs to get the thoughts out of my head, to heal my broken heart.

Three I Digging through Memories

Again I find myself home alone, and not able to sleep.

Leaning back on a pillow on my bed, sipping on a bottle of Jack Daniels I'm scrolling through facebook on my phone.

As always that's a bad idea, especially when a memory pops up in my feed of a day Anni and I went to the zoo.

We'd driven to the city together in my Ute, risking the trip as I wasn't even on my p's at the time and getting a fine would have been a huge mistake.

The day had been hot, even with the aircon cranked in the car sweat dripped down our foreheads and necks. Anni was wearing her hair in a ponytail and curly tendrils that had escaped were clinging to her cheeks and neck.

In every picture, she looked absolutely gorgeous and so happy.

It makes me think about where I went wrong in our relationship, as moments like the ones in the pictures filling my newsfeed were perfect and I curse myself for ever thinking the whole friends with benefits thing was ever a good idea.

Annika had a good heart, she was always so caring and loving. I knew it was selfish to take advantage of that nature but I'd done it and broke my own heart in the process. She'd told me at the beginning of our arrangement that one of us would fall in love, but I didn't expect that someone to be me.

Anni had pulled me in, being with her completely, living with her, it was all so perfect and I fell hard; so hard it hurt like a bitch when she didn't fall with me. It still hurts; her leaving is making me feel empty and looking back on old memories is like a stab in the heart, repeatedly over and over again telling me 'look you were happy Austin, look what you lost, you fucked up big time.'

Closing the last photo on my phone, I wipe my arm across my tear stained cheeks, trying to sniff back more tears when Bella appears in my doorway.

"Austin, are you ok? I could hear your sobbing when I came in."

I hold my phone up to her, stuttering, "I'm f...f..fine."

"Well, it doesn't look like it. Why are you showing me your phone?"

"Pictures of Anni and I came up in my newsfeed," I reply, sniffing back more tears again.

"Oh...ok...and you looked at them and got upset?"

"What does it look like Bel?" I snap, annoyed at her question.

She laughs, walking across the room and sitting on the edge of the bed next to me.

"I know its hard Aust, but you gotta move on."

"Easier said than done, Bel."

"I know, but..."

"But what Bel?"

"I could..."

I'm about to reply when she grabs my neck leaning against me as she presses a kiss to my lips. She smiles against my mouth, running her hands along my jaw as she deepens the kiss.

Still kissing me, she climbs onto my lap, her knees on either side of my thighs. Her hands still graze my jaw and neck as we kiss; my hands starting to entangle in her hair.

Bella is definitely an amazing kisser, knowing exactly how to make my body react.

Hitching her mini-skirt up she grinds against my groin, again kissing me before she pulls back to ask, "Aust, are you sure we should?"

Caz May

"Seriously Bel, can't you feel my cock against you right now?"

She doesn't reply, instead grabs the waistband of my shorts yanking them down to find I'm commando.

She runs her hands over my length, about to lean down and take me in her mouth when I shake my head, "I just want to fuck you, Bel."

"Fine, get a franger out," she demands, smirking at me when I open the drawer, reaching in and getting a condom out to hand to her without looking.

Ripping it open, she slides it easily onto my cock.

Reaching between her legs, she touches herself as she shifts the minimal fabric of her g-string aside before lowering her body onto my cock.

Slowly, agonisingly good, she rocks up and down, almost slipping right off before pushing down all the way again.

I'd hardly ever fucked Anni cowgirl, and watching Bella ride my cock turns me on so much.

Grabbing her by the waist I pull her down to kiss me, forcing my cock deeper inside her.

As our lips dance together, she moans as I take her tongue with mine.

I can feel my climax building, a quick hot spurt filling the latex between us.

Taking my mouth from hers, I taunt, "Don't come, Bel, I want to taste you."

"Aust...I...I don't think that's a good idea."

"Why?"

"I...I don't know. It..it just..."

Pouting, I tease, "Pretty please Bel...I wanna lick your cherry and taste your cream."

Laughing she playfully slaps my arm, before pulling herself off my cock and moving up over my chest so her clit is at my lips, ready to take between my teeth.

Biting the sensitive bud she hisses, grabbing the headboard and grinding her pelvis against my face.

Lowering my tongue to her slit, I push my tongue inside her folds as she bucks against my face.

She starts to moan, as I delve deeper, licking all the cream she's offering.

I smile against her when she begins to shudder, her release sudden over my face, "Oh fuck Aust!"

Moving back she blushes when I tease, "Bel, you just squirted all over my face, you dirty girl."

Again she playfully slaps me, "Don't Aust ok. I...I..."

"What? You always squirt when you get given an Aussie kiss?"

"Um....", she blushes, biting her lip as she looks at me like the cat got her tongue.

"Fuck Bel, that's hot as."

"No, it's not....it's embarrassing."

"Trust me, Bel, it's hot and you know what's even hotter?"

She shakes her head, so I reply, taunting her, "You kissing me after."

"Aust please," she protests with a smile on her face that betrays her protest.

"Kiss me, Bella," I demand grabbing her cheeks to pull her down to my lips.

As our lips touch, she moans, licking her cream from my lips and thrusting her tongue into my mouth.

I'd thought she was a great kisser before but now her kiss is wild and all I want is more of whatever I can get from Bella.

The pleasure of being with her blocks out all the pain of not being with Anni.

Four | She said Hi

Bella

Even though I've just had coffee, I feel like a zombie as I drag my sorry butt home from meeting up with Anni. Telling her about being with Austin again is weighing on my mind. I'm not sure if telling her was really as good of an idea as it seemed when the words left my mouth at her question.

I know taking advantage of him being upset, basically just using him for sex is wrong; but I've just needed to feel and block out the heartbreak of how things ended with Jace. We'd both brought about the demise of our relationship, but unlike him when I'd cheated I was tanked, not sober.

He'd made a choice, and even though I'd made a choice too, I wasn't thinking straight.

I can't say that now though, as the last time I slept with Austin I was completely aware of my actions and it was a mistake.

A mistake that I had to shake away of how good it felt to be with him, sober.

I don't want to develop feelings for anyone, as feelings lead to heartbreak. Any feelings directed towards Austin would be total heart anarchy.

Walking into the apartment I find Austin busily cooking something in the kitchen.

As soon as the smell wafts towards me as I enter the kitchen it's evident he is cooking something that Anni loved to eat; pancakes.

Sitting down at the breakfast bar I chastise him, "You have to stop this Austin. It's kinda pathetic."

"It's not pathetic to want to remember Bella," he protests waving a spatula at me when he turns around to meet my eyes.

"It is when it's taking over your life Austin. She's been gone for weeks."

"Yeah I know that Bella," he defends, flipping the pancake before wiping his arm across his face, "and I miss her like crazy."

"Then contact her. Tell her how you're feeling."

"I can't Bella," he protests again, shaking the whipped cream can, "she doesn't want to speak to me."

"You don't know that Austin. She asked about you."

He squeezes a large swirl of whipped cream over his pancakes before grabbing a spoon out of the drawer and taking in a big mouthful.

After swallowing a few bites, he sighs, "You know she made it pretty clear she didn't want to speak to me the day she left and when we had that fight."

"That might have been true but..."

He waves the spoon towards me, cutting me off, "But what Bella? She misses me huh?"

"Yes, she told me today that she misses you and said to say 'hi'."

He smiles wide, before taking another bite and replying, "That's nice but don't reply back, ok?"

"Why? It'd be obvious to a blind man that you miss her like crazy!"

"I do miss her, so fucking bad but I don't know."

"Don't know what Austin? I'm not following what's going through your carrot-topped head right now."

"I just feel like even though she asked about me she doesn't even care."

"You know Anni will always care about you and has asked about you because she does care."

"Hmmm, yeah I guess. Did you tell her about us?"

"Yeah," I pout, the regret surfacing in my mind again, "shouldn't I have?"

"No Bella!" He screams at me, "We're not together!"

"I know that Austin! You've made that clear."

"Oh really? So you don't want me either?"

"No, I don't. You seem to like friends with benefits arrangements."

He frowns, his words through clenched teeth like a bite, "Don't be a bitch Bella!"

"I'm not Austin," I reply defensively crossing my arms across my chest.

"Whatever! Leave me alone," he snaps, throwing his empty bowl in the sink before heading off towards his bedroom.

Digging my phone out of my pocket I send Anni a text.

Bel: Austin is an idiot

Anni: hey bel...why do you say that?

Bel: he misses you like crazy...he was cooking pancakes when I got home

Anni: oh right....did you tell him I said hi?

Bel: yeah and he didn't want you to know he says hi back

Anni: ok um I guess he's an idiot then

Bel: yep an idiot still in love with you

Anni: um yeah bel I gotta go Jai just got home ;)

I don't bother replying, knowing she'll be busy now her gorgeous boyfriend has arrived home to their penthouse.

It's hard to admit to myself, but I'm insanely jealous of my friend. Anyone would have to have be a complete idiot to not know that I had a mega crush on Jairus.

But from the first day I met him, I could see he only had eyes for Anni and I'd never of had a chance with him.

My decisions of late when it came to guys were nothing short of idiotic; sleeping with Austin the most idiotic decision of them all.

I need space from all guys, but short of moving back home with Mum, I have nowhere to go.

Five | I'm Not Her

Bella

I've been in one of those half asleep, half awake kind of dozing periods of sleep and wake up feeling like I've actually climaxed.

The giddy feeling passes quickly when my bedroom door cracks open.

Austin stumbles in clearly drunk and high as a kite. He's giggling like a kid but is barely standing up. I wonder how he even knew how to make it home as he clearly isn't in a right state of mind.

Stumbling across the room, he falls into a heap at the bottom of my bed. Crawling up the sheets towards me, his fingers brush my bare skin making me squirm and giggle.

"Mmm...so um ike at," he says, not even forming full words.

He reaches my head, trying to press a kiss to my lips as he rocks his pelvis over mine.

"Aust! Seriously you reek of jack and weed," I screech at him.

"Mmm...but Anni I need you," he moans, his words a little clearer.

"Austin I'm not Annika! Get out of my room!"

"Anni's room," he corrects, laughing like a hyena.

"No Austin. My room, I'm Bella."

He laughs again, a lustful look in his eyes when my words register in his brain.

"Mmm Bella; you're my friend with benefits."

I shift in the bed, pushing his body off mine, "Austin please just go to bed."

He again laughs, giving me another whiff of the jack and weed on his breath, "Let me in your bed Bella." He's again slurring his words as he tries to touch me.

I can't make out what he is actually saying but I know it's something sexual and there is no way I'm going to sleep with him again whilst he's drunk, not to mention stoned.

Instead, I reach across to slap him, to hopefully knock some sense into him. He screeches in pain, sitting up on the bed next to me.

"Fine!" he snaps, as he stands up to stumble out of the room without even a backwards glance.

As soon as he closes the door behind him, I grab my phone from the bedside table to send a text.

Bella: Jax...are you still living with Jace?

Jaxon: No...why? whats up babe?

Bella: I need a place to stay for a couple of days

Jaxon: Yeah sure...when?

Bella: Like right now

Jaxon: Im not home now babe...tomorrow?

Bella: Ok text me your addy in the morning?

Jaxon: no worries babe..you're not in danger are you?

Bella: no nothing like that....just need some space from my roomie

Jaxon: what roomie? Didn't they move out?

Bella: two of them did yeah...I'll tell ya tomorrow

Jaxon: alright babe...talk to ya later

Putting my phone down, I think about if going to stay with Jaxon is a good idea considering our past history.

But I trust him, as even though he's part of the reason I broke up with his twin brother he'd always been there to listen to any problem I was facing.

I hate admitting to myself too that I actually think Jax is the hotter of the brothers, and I kinda always wanted him to be my boyfriend, not Jace.

Jaxon always seemed to have a girlfriend though, or a least a girl he was 'seeing' as he put it and until that night we slept together he'd never dared to make a move on his brother's girlfriend.

Part of me now feels like maybe I'm going to end up with Jaxon in the end like I'd always wanted, but my mind is confused as sleeping with Austin has brought up feelings from the past and I know that seeing Jaxon again is going to confuse me even more.

There is only one other person who'd understand how confused I'm feeling, as she'd been in the exact same situation mere months ago; but I don't want to break her blissful new relationship honeymoon bubble with my crappy love life dramas.

I hate lying to Anni, but I've had to do it a lot in the past year, firstly about my mega crush on Jairus and now having feelings for Austin again. I'm not sure if she'd even care if I did get with Austin, but I know it isn't right. I want them to be best friends again, and him being my boyfriend would make that even more complicated.

My eyes are closing, as the word complicated tumbles in my head. My love life is most definitely complicated.

Six | Waking up stoned

It's past midday when I finally wake, my head pounding from the after-effects of too much alcohol and a weed-induced high.

Stumbling into the kitchen to make coffee, I'm hoping to find Bella home. It's Saturday though and she normally works on the weekends so it isn't really odd that she's not home. But being past midday she was sometimes home as her shifts were generally morning ones.

My head feels so groggy like a bus has hit me straight between the eyes. There isn't even enough coffee left in the jar for a decent cup. I curse myself for not remembering to get some when I was at the supermarket.

Me and shopping for groceries didn't really go together, I'd go in for one thing and leave without that very thing; this week that item was coffee.

It makes me think of Anni, as she was always so organised when it came to food shopping. She'd go with a list, categorised by the exact aisle it was in. She also stacked the trolley and conveyor belt exactly as she wanted it packed into the bags so nothing broke and all the cold items were together.

As there is no coffee I decide to have a shower. In the bathroom, I turn the taps to halfway, not scolding hot but not freezing. Steam rises through the bathroom, as I undress from my pyjama daks.

My morning wood is still prominent and stepping under the water I let it cascade over my naked body. Thinking about Anni has only made my morning wood even more prominent.

Leaning back against the shower wall, the water is now falling directly over my aching crotch, as I grab it between a fist.

As thoughts of the Saturday night, I fucked Anni in the shower surface in my mind, I pump my hand up and down my cock.

Closing my eyes, I can't help but scream out her name imagining her dainty soft hands are wrapped around my cock instead of my callous ones.

With a final pump, my warm cum spurts out, covering my hand in the sticky white liquid.

Sighing I wash it off under the warm water before sliding down my arse to the floor.

I can feel the tears stinging my cheeks. They are partly because I miss her, partly because I've just jacked off thinking about the hottest sex we ever had and partly because I'm wondering if I should find a way to contact her.

Standing up, I let the water fall over my body again, grabbing the loofah and crappy Lynx Africa body wash that has been in the shower forever.

As I run the soapy bubbles over my abs, I curse myself remembering that I deleted Anni's number from my phone, afraid I'd drunk dial her.

Washing off the soap from my body, I make a mental note to ask Bella for it when she returns home.

Turning off the taps, I grab a towel from the rack, dragging it over my body quickly before pulling my pyjama daks back on.

Heading to the lounge room, I flop down on the couch, content to play the Switch for the arvo.

~~

When my stomach starts growling, telling me I've not eaten all day I drag myself off the couch to make Kraft Mac & Cheese, chicken flavoured.

Checking my phone as I wait for it to cook I see it's half past seven. It worries me a little that Bella still hasn't come home but as the microwave dings I shrug it off.

Friends Don't Say Goodbye

She's a grown woman, and not my girlfriend so I
really have no business worrying about her.
After eating my Mac & Cheese, throwing my plate in
the sink I go into her room to sleep in her bed.

Seven | Bad girl Beautiful

Bella

Looking at the address on my phone after work, I'm
still hesitant if going to Jax's house is a good idea.
He's living on the other side of the city, in Pascoe Vale
and I'm nervous getting on a train line I don't know.
I'm also nervous about seeing Jax again as well. We'd
text each other a bit, but I'd not seen him since the
day I found out about Jace cheating and we'd gotten
back together. He'd not been around when I'd gone
over to Jace's and that was good and bad.
Taking a deep sigh I step up onto Jax's doorstep,
pressing the doorbell and hearing it reverberate
through the house.

My heart is pounding hard in my chest. I'm about to
turn away and run back to the footpath; whilst
cursing myself for this stupid idea when the door
cracks open.
Jax stands against it, in black trackie daks and a loose
white t-shirt. He smiles when he sees me, my black
work outfit of jeggings and a v-neck fitted t-shirt not
hiding anything from his wandering gaze.

"Hey babe," he drawls, his smirk growing wider when I feel myself blush.

"Hi Jax," I reply, not sure whether to hug him or shake his hand.

"You ok?" He asks, stepping back from the door, ushering me inside.

His hand brushes the small of my back, sending a shiver up my spine.

Swallowing the lump in my throat, as he closes the door behind us, I reply, "Not really."

"Bel, I don't like seeing you upset," he offers, showing me towards the inviting couch in his lounge room.

"I'm not upset Jax...it's just he's like a...god I don't even know," I laugh, gulping.

"Who babe?"Jax asks, sitting down on the couch, patting the empty spot next to him.

I stand there a moment, not sure if I should sit next to him when I'm feeling a strange sense of attraction to him.

Sighing though I sit down, trying to keep as much distance as I can without him noticing.

"So who's got you all riled up babe? I know it's not my brother."

"No, it's Austin."

"Your roomie?"

"Yeah, he's fucking pining after Anni and won't leave me alone. He only wants sex and I've had it!"

"Sounds crazy," he replies with a half-hearted laugh that stirs an odd feeling in my stomach, "What else has happened?"

I blurt out everything to him, watching as his expression changes when I tell him about telling Jace and that after we both cheated everything went downhill.

"God, my brother is such a fucking dickhead, Bel. I'm sorry."

"Don't be Jax.I'm the one who should be sorry but I didn't know who else I could talk to."

"All good babe," he replies smirking at me again, "I'm always here for you."

His voice is laced with a sentiment in that promise that makes my stomach flip flop when I reply,

"Thanks, Jax. I'm really sorry about what happened with Jace too."

"Why Bella?" He asks, almost laughing.

"Because we hurt him, Jax."

"Yeah but he's got a new girlfriend now," he laughs, before biting down on his lips when he looks at me and the sad look I know is plastered on my face.

"Oh really?" I ask, intrigued and a little hurt.

"It's probably one of the girls he cheated on you with and you deserve better Bella."

Again his voice is laced with the same sweet tone.

"Thanks but maybe I'm not the relationship kinda girl," I muse, feeling my heart thump in my chest, telling me my words are lies, "I just want an honest guy you know?"

"Yeah," he muses looking at me lustfully.

"What Jax?" I laugh.

"You're fucking gorgeous Bel," he drawls, moving closer to me on the couch so that when he leans forward his lips are almost on mine.

"Jax stop! We can't!" I protest, even though I can feel my body telling me the complete opposite.

Pressing his forehead against mine he asks, "Why not?"

"Because we can't," I whisper against his lips, that I want against mine.

"That's not an answer Bella," he replies before kissing me, softly at first and then harder when I moan and shift on the couch as a rush of pleasure races through me.

Breaking the kiss, I muse in a husky tone, "Jax?"

"Yeah?" He groans.

"Kiss me again," I taunt.

He moans, pushing my body down onto the couch as he takes my mouth with his in another hot kiss.

This kiss is more demanding than before, more teasing as his tongue runs along my lips forcing them to part.

Biting down on my tongue he lets out the most delicious moan, making my underwear dampen even more. I've kissed Jax before, but it's never made me feel so aroused.

Breaking the kiss, I moan, "Mmm, Jax."

"Bel," he drawls, licking his lips, "I want to fuck you so bad right now."

"Jax, we shouldn't but...." I start before he cuts my words off by plunging his hand into the front of my jeggings.

"Mmm, Bel you're soaked babe," he moans grabbing my crotch through the cotton of my knickers.

"Jax stop, please. We can't have sex right now."

Taking his hand out of my daks, he licks his fingers smirking, "And why the hell not Bella?"

"Because it's all kinds of wrong Jaxon," I taunt back using his full name for effect as well.

"And all kinds of right Bella. For once I'd like to fuck you sober."

The smirk is still on his face, as he pulls his t-shirt over his head, positioning himself over me with his hands on either side of my hips. His chest isn't quite as defined as his brothers, and his love handles are prominent but he's still gorgeous.

My heart starts to hammer in my chest, as he looks down at me smiling.

I know even thinking about sleeping with him is wrong, but my aching crotch is having other ideas and I'm wondering if it would different when we are sober.

Teasingly I run a finger down the middle of his chest, loving how his skin heats at the simple touch. He has a small snail trail of hair below his belly button leading into his daks and teasingly as I touch the soft hair, I whisper, "I wonder where this leads."

"Bel, please babe," he begs, grabbing the hem of my t-shirt in his hands, "Can I take this off?"

Nodding I lift my arms above my head and he edges the t-shirt up and over my head.

"God, Bel, you're so fucking sexy."

Playfully I slap his arm, "You're only saying that to get in my daks."

"Is it working?"

"Maybe," I tease, my fingers grazing the elastic of his trackies.

There is silence between us for a moment, our breathing growing rapid as we look at each half naked like it's the first time we've ever been in this situation together.

He again leans over my body to kiss me, sending the ache to my crotch again. Wrapping my arms around him and entangling my hands in his hair I pull him closer against my body, taking his mouth as mine and loving the feeling of his cock hardening.

Breaking this kiss he taunts, "Bel, you made my cock hard."

"Yeah, it looks that way," I taunt, dakking him.

His cock springs free from his boxers as I yank them down to his knees.

I gasp seeing him fully erect, again that feeling of it being like the first time we've been together crossing my mind. He kisses my belly button, running his tongue along the sensitive skin of my hips.

"So Bel, if I dak you what's going to happen?" he taunts smirking.

"I don't know Jax. Do it and find out," I tease back, lifting my hips off the couch as he yanks my jeggings and knickers down all at once.

Running a finger along my slit he teases, "Mmm Bel, you wax babe."

I giggle when his finger reaches my clit, "Yeah and..."

"It's hot! I can see your pussy so much better," he teases, pushing a finger inside me.

Laughing I reply, "Don't refer to my vagina as that word again or I won't let you fuck me."

"Oh really?" he laughs, taking out his finger and licking it clean.

I don't reply, biting my lip instead, watching him taste my arousal on his finger.

His eyes close as he moans, "Mmm, Bel. You taste divine."

Again, I don't reply but pull him down to kiss him, hard and zealously. I want his kiss all over my body and it's scaring the shit out of me, but arousing me at the same time.

"Jax?" I drawl his name, breaking the kiss, panting.

"Yeah Bel?"

"I want your kiss all over."

He growls, "Bella, are you asking me for an Aussie kiss?"

"Yes," I moan, as he licks down my body, deliberately stopping when he reaches my hips.

Resting his head on my hips he looks up at me with a sinful smirk on his face. I know I'm asking for trouble with my request, but I want to feel, want to let go again and again.

Before I can think another thought about how wrong being with my ex's brother is, he presses his lips against my clit, sending the rush of pleasure through me again. Even though it hasn't been long since Austin had gone down on me,I've almost forgotten how amazing it feels.

His tongue delves lower, lapping up my arousal like it's the most delicious thing he's ever tasted.

My hips buck up to his face, as his tongue runs over my clit again, sending me closer to the edge.

Still nibbling my clit, he pushes a finger inside me, pressing against my walls to tease the magic spot.

Gripping the couch with my palms, I moan as my climax rips through my body, a wave that makes me shiver and release harder than I have in months.

Jax licks my folds again, before stretching up over my body and smirking at me like the cat who tasted the cream.

"God Bella. Why have I never given you an Aussie before?"

"Um...maybe because I was your brother's girlfriend."

He laughs, "True, but that didn't stop us from fucking."

"Yeah, and Jax?"

"Yeah?" he asks, still with the smirk on his face.

"That was the best Aussie kiss ever, but...."

"Thanks," he laughs, "but what?"

"I want you to fuck me now, please."

"You don't need to say please Bel," he laughs, pressing his cock against my entrance as he kisses me. It turns me on more tasting myself on his tongue.

When he breaks the kiss, he's frowning, "Um Bel, I actually don't have any frangers in the house."

"Don't worry about it Jax."

"But Bel...I...I"

I laugh, "No I meant don't worry about it and just fuck me bare."

The smirk appears on his face again and not replying he slides inside me.

He again lets out the delicious moan, starting to thrust in and out.

"God, Bel," he moans,"was...it...this...good...last...time?"

Wrapping my legs around his arse I pull him deeper, "No, fuck Jax, you feel so good inside me."

His thrusts are harder, plunging deeper and hitting my g-spot again with the tip of his cock.

Leaning over my body again, he kisses me so hard I feel breathless and moan against his mouth to get some air.

Being with him drunk was nothing on being with him sober and pulling him deeper with my legs I buck my hips up to meet his thrusts.

"Jax! Jax! Fuck Jax!" I scream out as another heavenly climax rushes through my body.

"God, Bella, you look so gorgeous when you cum."
A blush rises up my cheeks and he smiles wickedly as he pulls out of my body, grabbing his cock in his fist releasing his load over my stomach.

Grabbing his t-shirt he wipes it away before he stretches over me to kiss me again.

"Bel, that was a serious ripper fuck."

I laugh, "Yeah so much better when we're sober."

Sitting up he pulls up his daks awkwardly, looking across at me as I do the same.

"Bel, I'm not going to be able to keep my hands off you if you stay here."

I smile at him, crawling on my knees to be closer to him again.

Kissing him I reply, "Better go get some franger's then Jax."

"Bel, really? Are you sure? I feel like I'm taking advantage of you."

"Why would you think that?"

"You just needed a place to stay, someone to talk to and I...I fuck you instead."

"I'm not complaining Jax."

He laughs, tipping his head back as he swallows making his Adam's apple bob.

"Me either Bel. I've always kinda had a crush on you."

I know shock crosses my face when he blushes, "Really?"

"Yeah."

"Well, I kinda always thought you were hotter than Jace."

"Is that so?"

"Yep," I laugh straddling him and kissing him again. Thoughts are tumbling in my head that maybe staying with him is beyond crazy, but the way he'd just made me feel twice is winning out.

Sex with Austin is good, but sex with Jaxon is something else entirely and I wonder if maybe being with him now is going to be the start of something amazing.

Eight | Dull Monotonous Days

Mondays are seriously the worst day of the week. This year they were made even worse by having back to back lectures from Nine am in the fucking morning until after Noon.

Sitting in my final lecture of the day, Coding, I'm trying to focus on the professors dribble whilst drawing on the lecture pad in front of me.
I should be writing notes, as coding in third year is beyond complicated but instead, my lecture pad now has a boxing kangaroo scrawled all over it.
It's a pretty decent drawing, and giving myself a mental pat on the back for the effort I stifle a laugh as my mind wanders to everything else going on in my life.
Things just feel so dull and boring, the days passing by in a blur of everyday monotony.
It's like I'm asking too much for wanting something exciting to happen and I'm missing things like the nights in with Anni playing board games. It seems stupid to miss something so lame, and so far from

exciting but it's what I miss most about my best friend being absent from my life.

It doesn't help that Bella hasn't been home either.

The house feels so lonely without another person around, so much so I've contemplated getting a dog.

I've tried texting her but she's ignoring my texts, leaving every one I send on 'read'.

It fucking hurts, like a stab in the guts. She's only a friend, a fuck buddy so to speak, but I hate being ignored.

The clock finally ticks over to the next hour, and the professor claps his hands together in a weird gesture, announcing that's we all have time for today.

I've never been gladder to get out of somewhere and gathering my items I run out of the lecture theatre at breakneck speed, even though I have nowhere to go until boxing at four.

In my rush, I bump into a pretty brunette on her way into the lecture theatre. Our books fly everywhere and she lets out a flustered sigh, as I scoop them up handing them back to her. She smiles at me in thanks but she doesn't say anything.

Looking at her closer as we both stand up, a moment of recollection flashes in my mind that I've seen her before, but I can't place where and I shrug it off as she walks away.

Her hand brushes mine, as she enters the lecture theatre and I'm surprised at the familiar jolt that runs through my body.

She's certainly pretty, in a different way to Anni, obviously being brunette, but also more so than Bella in a way I just can't explain.

~~

After grabbing a greasy box of goodness at Kentucky Fried Chicken for lunch I wander around the city for a bit, eyeing off some rad multicoloured Converse in Platypus shoes before I head to boxing.

Shoving my bag in my locker I grab my gloves out, pulling them on after stripping from my t-shirt.
I'd worn black fleecy Adidas trackie daks so I'd not have to change fully.
Out in the main room, I spot Kaden near the punching bags, laying into one like he's imagining he's hitting his worst enemy.
Stepping up at the bag next to him I punch it so hard he stops dead and glares at me.
"You ok mate? You boxed that hard."
"Not really," I confess, laying into the punching bag even harder as it swings back at me.

"Why? What's going on mate?"

"I miss Anni and Bella hasn't been home for like a week."

He laughs, his hands gripping the bag as it swings back.

I look at him when he speaks again, "Sounds like you're missing the sex mate."

"Yeah but I've gotta stop thinking with my knob," I laugh halfheartedly, wiping my arm across my brow, "having a fuck buddy isn't all its cracked up to be."

"You falling for Bella now too?" he laughs, with a jeering tone in his voice.

"Nah she's not my type."

Again he laughs, licking his lips when he asks, "So skank is not your type?"

"Come on mate, she's not a skank....Oh just forget it," I snap, upset that he could imply something like that about Bella when he's not officially met her.

He'd been at our party last year but I'd not actually had the chance to introduce them.

He only knew Bella by looks, and what I'd confided after we slept together.

Again I punch the bag hard, taking out all my frustration with my fists.

Kaden has gone back to hitting his own bag but glances over at me every few seconds like he still wants to say something or knows I want to say something else that is teetering on the tip of my tongue.

He stops again, grabbing his bag to stop it from swinging, asking breathlessly, "Is that all that's bothering you, Aust?"

"No Kaden, but I um....I..." stutter, about to mention the pretty brunette when coach calls out "Austin, get into the ring now. Your big match is coming up."

Kaden calls out to my back as I flip on the ropes into the ring, "Tell me later Austin. I gotta go get ready for my date."

Sticking my tongue out at him as he wanders off, he flips the bird in response and I laugh so hard my stomach hurts.

Kaden is a good mate, not my best friend but the closest friend I have at the moment and for that I'm grateful.

Nine | Under the covers

Jaxon

Bella has been staying with me for a little over a week. She'd not disclosed much about why she didn't really want to go home.

There was no complaining from me having her in my one bedroom apartment though, as she'd come back from work, walking in the door immediately stripping to her underwear.

As I'd said to her I'd not been able to keep my hands off her and we'd practically fucked in every inch of my apartment. My favourite places being the kitchen bench and the couch.

She'd had to borrow my underwear as she'd soaked hers the day she came apart on the couch.

If it was even possible Bella looked more tempting wearing my tightey whitey jocks than her own skimpy underwear.

Sighing she walks in the door again, immediately lifting the black t-shirt she'd also borrowed over her head. Slipping the jeggings down her legs, kicking them aside she looks at me with a teasing smile.

Smirking at her I purse my lips, wanting to grab her to push her to the floor and fuck her right there and then.

Stepping a little closer, she coos seductively, "Oh hey Jax."

"Mmm, hey Bel," I drawl, chuckling under my breath. "What Jax?"

"Nothing, you just look super sexy in my jocks."

"Oh, um, okay."

Running my fingertips up her arm suggestively I purr her name, "Bel."

She shivers, snatching her arm away and reaching up to pull her hair off her face.

"Jax....I...um...need..."

"Tell me, Bel...you don't need to hide anything from me."

"I ah...need to go home."

"I know, but at least just stay tonight," I suggest, finding it hard to not just pull her into my arms to kiss her senseless.

She's made me feel something I've not felt before with any other girl, and it's scaring the bejeezus out of me.

I'm not in love with her, but the sex is so damn good.

It's like a drug I can't get enough of.

"Jax....I...um don't know if I should....I..."

Not meaning to I snap at her, "Why not Bella?"

"Because...this....us....it's so wrong Jax," she muses folding her arms across her chest to cover her cleavage.

"And why is that Bella?"

"You know why Jaxon. If Jace found out he'd probably kill you."

"Yeah true, but Bel you can't deny we're good together. Better than good actually."

"I'm not denying that the sex is great Jax...but I..."

"Spit it out Bella, or I'm just going to kiss you."

"I told you the other day I want an honest guy."

Scowling I shake my head, "I know, and not telling my brother about us isn't exactly being honest."

"Exactly Jax," She affirms walking across the room to the kitchen and bending down as she opens the fridge.

My jocks stretch across her arse and gulping I cross the kitchen, stepping up behind her.

Leaning into her back, I kiss under her ear and she exhales a shaky breath.

Caz May

In her ear, I whisper seductively, "Just spend one more night with me, babe."

Sighing as she turns around, she pushes her hands against my bare chest to move my body forward and the fridge closes behind her.

"Jax I don't think we should."

"Please Bel, I want to bury my cock inside you again."

She moans, recalling how good we are together under the covers.

When she bites down on her lips, I let out a growl cupping her cheeks in my palms and smashing my lips against hers.

As she kisses me, she purrs my name seductively against my lips.

It sends my cock rising and I grab her around the waist. Wrapping her arms around my neck she jumps up to then wrap her legs around my back, still kissing me so hard I can barely breathe.

It makes me feel so turned on like I've never been kissed before and I never want to kiss anyone but her again.

Stepping backwards with our bodies still connected, after I break the kiss I tease, "You're going to ride my cock tonight babe."

Smirking at me when we back into my room, my knees bump into the edge of the bed and I fall back onto the tangle of sheets, bringing her down with me.

A thought flashes in my mind of whether we'd be good together outside the bedroom, but it's quickly dismissed when her lips are against mine again and she's kissing me like she isn't going to kiss me again.

My cock is aching, bulging at the front of my trackies just from kissing her. I know I'm in big trouble feeling this way about anyone, especially Bella but it's so euphoric and knowing she's going to be gone in the morning I give in.

Demanding entrance to her mouth with my tongue I deepen the kiss, tasting coffee and minties mixed together which I know is going to be a taste I crave.

As we kiss, her hands find my hair gripping it as she starts rocking her crotch over the bulge in my daks. It's sending my desire for her even higher. Slipping my hands in the back of the jocks, I grab her arse cheeks in my palms.

She moans against my mouth, pulling back as I edge them down. Smiling at me she lifts her hips up so I can push the jocks to her knees.

"Bel?"

"Yeah Jax?" she replies huskily.

"Can you take your bra off? I want to see you ride my cock naked."

Biting her lip, she doesn't reply but sitting up a little she reaches around her back to unhook the eyes and lets the bra fall down her arms to my chest.

Grabbing it she throws it aside and smirks at me so deviously my cock hardens more.

"God Bella, you're such a fucking knockout!" I taunt cupping her breasts in my hands, kneading them, teasing the sensitive buds to attention, making her moan and tip her head back.

"Oh Jax, that feels amazing."

Grinning I run a finger between her breasts, down her stomach straight over her hips and into her smooth wet core.

"Oh, Bel! Fuck! You're soaked again."

"Touch me please Jax," she begs.

Shaking my head at her I lift my pelvis up to meet hers, yanking my trackies down my legs awkwardly. Thankfully I've gone commando so my cock eagerly springs forward meeting her entrance the moment my daks are down.

Giggling she grabs the trackies, helping slide them down to my knees.

"I need to be inside you Bella, now," I demand.

Again she lets out the hottest sounding giggle ever, sliding down onto my cock as I push up against her.

She lets out a whimper of pleasure, as she starts bouncing up and down on my rock hard cock.

It has been way too long since any girl has fucked me cowgirl and it's absolute ecstasy feeling how she grips my cock inside her.

Bella is so vocal during sex as well, moaning and cursing as she rocks her body with mine.

Sitting up I wrap my arms around her back, forcing my cock deeper inside her. Smashing a kiss to her lips, I can feel my release building, knowing I need to pull out but also feeling so overwhelmed with lust that I know it's too late.

"Bel...I....ll...," I start to say, reality hitting my head that I'm about to say 'I love you' to Bella, to Bella the gorgeous brunette my brother stole from me even though he knew I had a mega crush on her in high school.

Bella who is currently riding my cock with such abandonment my feelings come crashing into mind as my release rocks my body, filling hers.

Her lips find mine, as her body shudders with her own release before we fall back against the bed panting, unable to move.

Once she's caught her breath, she leaps off me like a fire has started between us.

She pulls my jocks back up her legs, looking at me with an odd longing look on her face as she runs out of my bedroom.

I stand against the door jamb for a moment, watching her as she pulls on her jeggings and shrugs my t-shirt on.

"Bella, please don't go. I...II..."

She turns to look back at me, "Don't Jax....please don't say that....I have to go."

Slinging her bag over her shoulder, I watch her open the door to leave without another look back at me. Sinking to the floor, I curse myself for one letting her stay in the first place but mostly for the fact that I'd fucked her and being with her made the feelings come crashing back.

The sex with Bella is good, so fucking good, and I'm a complete idiot because I don't want to be without her.

Denial is plaguing me now, as there is no way I can really be in love with Bella.

My head is telling me one thing, but the pounding of my heart is telling me another.

Ten | A Personal Manifestation

Being in a house alone makes me so anxious,
jumping and almost screaming at every little creak of
the walls or the wail of the wind outside.
I don't miss Bella so much, but just miss the company
and knowing someone else is in the house with me,
especially on a night when a summer storm is
battering the house.

Not able to sleep, as the thunder shakes the walls
and the rain pelts down on the roof, I'm sitting on the
couch listening to the storm with a beer in hand.
My mind is wandering back to nights at home when
Lily would crawl into my bed during a thunderstorm.
I'd stroke her hair and sing to her, calming her
beating heart.
Being away from my little sister is one of the things I
missed most about being away from home.
Grabbing my phone I dial her number.
Even though it's after nine pm she answers eagerly.
"Hey, big bro."
"Hey Lil, I miss you."

"Oh, Austy I miss you too. Christmas was forever ago."

"I know Lil. How's school?"

"Bleh, year twelve is so hard, Austy."

"I know Lil, but you're smarty pants. You'll do fine."

"Yeah, I hope so. Is that thunder I can hear?"

"Yeah, Lil. Huge storm going on and it made me miss you."

"Aww big bro, you're so cute."

"Don't laugh at me, Lil. I miss those times when you needed me."

"I know Austy. I miss you a lot too. I gotta go empty the fecking dishwasher. Mum's been a real b lately."

"That's no good Lil," I laugh knowing that Mum was always a bit of a tyrant when it came to chores, so now Lily would be picking up all the slack without myself and Amanda at home.

"Ok Austy, I'm hanging up now," she coos making a kissing sound into the phone, "bye big bro. I love you millions!"

"Bye Lil, love you trillions!" I reply, hearing her giggle as she hangs up the phone.

After hanging up a loud clap of thunder shakes the house, just as the front door bursts open and a

dishevelled, drenched Bella comes crashing in
cursing.

My eyes lock on her, as she drops her bag by the
door and heads to the kitchen.

It seems as though she is a world away, not saying a
word to me even when I enter the kitchen leaning on
the bench as she makes a coffee.

It looks as though she's been crying, but it could also
have been from the wet tendrils of her hair that are
clinging to the side of her face.

"Bel, where have you been?"

"Why do you care Austin?"

"I don't really, but it's storming big time out there,
plus I've been texting you and you haven't replied to
me."

"So," she snaps, pouring the hot water from the
kettle into her cup, "big fucking deal Austin!"

"I've been worried about you Bel, and now you come
home in the middle of this storm."

"If you must know I've been staying with a friend."

"Anni?" I ask intrigued.

"No not Anni and none of your business, Austin," she
spits at me, my full name like poison on her tongue.

"A guy?" I enquire.

"Austin, drop it yeah?" she snaps, taking a sip of her coffee.

Laughing I ask, "A new boyfriend then?"

"No!" she shouts a little too quickly, almost spitting out the coffee she just swallowed, "and if I did I'd not tell you anyway."

"Why are you being such a bitch?"

"Well, um, I've got something on my mind, but also because being around you lately Austin is stifling."

"Maybe, but you haven't exactly been around much. I'm fucking lonely Bel."

"So, you need to get a fucking life Austin."

I feel a pang of sadness hit me with her words,

"Without Anni, I don't have a life."

Bella's expression changes when she asks, "Seriously what's going on with you?"

"What do you mean? You know exactly what's going on with me Bella."

"No, I meant you've never been such a sad sack of shit. Since Anni left you've been so down in the fucking dumps and you're not even trying to do anything about being friends with her again."

"I can't Bella. She made it pretty clear that she hates me and I can't stand seeing her with him."

"She doesn't hate you."

"That might be true but seeing her with him, so happy, It really fucking hurts."

"Yeah well, you made ya bed Austin."

"There you go being a bitch again. I don't get you, Bella."

Slamming her coffee cup on the bench she chuckles oddly, "What the fuck does that mean?"

"You, you're so cold towards me unless you're fucking me."

She blushes, biting her lip and I wonder for a moment if it's an invitation to kiss her and drag her to the bedroom.

"Um, yeah I um....never should have slept with you Austin."

"Ok, whatever."

"I'm sorry ok," she replies looking at me like she wants to say something else but doesn't have the words.

"Sorry for what?"

"I've fucked up big time Austin ok, and I'm going home to Mum's tomorrow morning on the first bus," she informs me, leaving the kitchen and heading to her bedroom.

I let her be for a few minutes before I follow, finding her door wide open as she stuffs clothes into a gym bag in a huff.

"Bel?"

"What Austin? Can't you just leave me alone?"

"Did I do something wrong?"

"No, I did Austin ok."

"You're not making any sense Bella."

She slumps down on the bed next to the bag, wiping her arm across her face as tears start to fall down her cheeks.

"Nothing makes sense Austin. I'm so confused," she sobs through her tears when I sit next to her on the bed putting an arm around her.

I'm expecting her to shrug out of my embrace, but instead, she melts into my hug and turns to look up at me.

"Confused about what exactly Bel?"

"Us...and..."

"And?" I ask, my heart jolts in my chest.

"I...ah...I...fuck," she mutters, looking at me with dark lust in her eyes.

"Tell me, Bel, please," I beg, caressing her cheek with the back of my hand.

"I can't Austin ok. I just can't."

"What can I do to make it better?"

"Nothing," she snaps, biting down on her lip again.

This time I don't hesitate to smash my lips to hers, kissing her hard wondering if there is an 'us' and our kisses and time between the sheets is more than just friends with benefits.

She moans against my mouth before pulling away, "Aust, please, we can't...we can't."

"Why not Bel?"

"Because I can't keep taking advantage of you Aust ok."

"You're not Bel."

"It feels like I am Austin, and I hate myself for that. I don't want to use you for sex Austin. You deserve more than that."

"Seriously Bel, what's up with you?" I ask, stumped by her sudden change in attitude towards sex.

"I wish I could explain but I can't," she muses standing up to continue stuffing things into her bag.

"Bel, can I at least drive you home tomorrow? I hate the thought of you getting the bus home alone when you're upset."

"It's fine Austin. I'll get the bus."

Standing up from the bed, I hug her from behind, whispering in her ear, "No Bella, I'm driving you home and I won't take any other answer than yes." Turning in my embrace, she looks up at me, a slight smile on her lips when she replies, "Ok Aust, but I just want you to drop me off. No coming inside the house. I don't want Elyse thinking there is anything going on between us."

"Fine, you have a deal," I laugh smirking at her, "but I only accept such deals that are sealed with a kiss."

She laughs at my tease, before crashing her lips against mine. Her deal-sealing kiss makes me wonder if I want more from her and if she is wondering the same thing but is too scared to feel anything for me like I am possibly feeling for her.

Eleven | The Road Home

Bella

I've always loved the smell in the air and the calmness after a big thunderstorm. Waking up early I stuff my toiletries into my bag, about to sneak out the door when I find Austin standing in the kitchen holding two thermos mugs of coffee in his hands.

"Ready to go Bel?" he asks, smirking at me, proud of himself that he'd had the same thought about leaving early.
I don't reply, only laugh, taking one of the coffee cups and sipping it.
With his free hand, he takes my hand with his to lead me out to his ute, so I don't have a chance to back away.
I'm not sure why he is so adamant about driving me the three hours to Ararat. I barely have a cent to my name and my credit card isn't the best option so even though being in a car with Austin for three hours is going to be small talk torture I let him lead the way.

Dropping my hand at the door, he grabs the ute keys and slings a small overnight bag over his shoulder.

I open the door, walking out to his ute parked on the curb outside our apartment.

"Where do I put my bag?"

"Under the tonneau cover Bel," he laughs, unclipping the ocky straps that hold the black fabric closed.

"What if it rains?" I ask stupidly.

"It's pretty much waterproof Bel," he laughs again, putting his bag in before grabbing mine from my tentative grip.

"Ok, um," I mutter, not sure of what I was even going to say.

I have a hundred thoughts tumbling in my head on constant repeat. They are mainly of the last few days I'd spent at Jax's.

Sex with Jax was amazing and even when it felt so incredibly wrong I wanted it, wanted, craved how being with him made my body feel.

My mind is so mixed up with feelings, as being with Austin more had made the feelings I had for him in high school surface again and when he's so sweet towards me, like offering to drive me home to Mum's I wonder if he is feeling the same as I am.

It isn't love, but something that makes me want him in my life somehow, even if it is just for some good sex.

Getting into his ute, I clip my seatbelt in, trying not to look over at him as he gets in and starts the engine. The odd tension between us is only making me feel more confused.

Sighing, I think about what to say as he slips the gears up, as we drive out onto a relatively quiet Bridge Road.

As he changes gears, slipping into third his fingers brush against my thigh, sending goosebumps across my skin.

"Aust....um...don't."

"What Bel?"

"Don't touch me please," I snap, not actually meaning my words.

He frowns when he replies, "Sorry I didn't mean to."

"It's ok. I just don't want things to be any more awkward than they already are between us."

"I get it Bel, but I'm not the one making things that way."

Again I let out a deep sigh, wishing the time would go faster and we'd be out on the highway closer to home.

"I'm sorry Austin. It's just I um..."

"Tell me, Bel, please."

"Fine...I really like being with you Aust but I'm really confused."

"Don't tell me you're falling for me Bel?" he laughs lightheartedly.

"No, I um don't think so, but I..."

"Bel, don't lie to me," he jeers, sliding the gears into fifth as he guns the engine after turning onto to the highway.

"I'm not Aust, but I need to tell you something."

"What?" he smirks, his hand now on my thigh edging up under my skirt.

"I had a crush on you in high school, before you got with Anni. I really wanted to get with you that night in my bedroom."

He squeezes my thigh when he replies, "Shit Bel, I um....I kinda knew that, but why are you telling me that now?"

"Because actually being with you has made me wonder if I still feel that way."

He gulps hard, pondering his next words.

"I um...Bel...I... don't feel that way about you. I just..."

"I know Aust...it's just sex."

"For me yeah...damn good sex Bel. But is it more for you?" he asks slipping a finger into my knickers, teasing me.

My breath hitches as he starts to rub his finger over my clit.

"No, Aust...its not...its..." I pant breathlessly as his finger slides inside me and I shift on the seat.

"It's what Bel?" he taunts, stopping his sweet torture for a moment.

"I slept with someone else and it was amazing, but he almost admitted that he was in love with me."

"And now you're confused about your feelings?"

"Yes," I reply meekly.

"Bel, being with you makes me feel good and helps block out my feelings, but if you don't want to any more I'll stop right now."

Smiling at him, I reply, "Um actually Aust I feel the same way and I kinda want to block out how I'm feeling too."

He again laughs, "So who'd you fuck Bel?"

"You'll think I'm an idiot if I tell you."

"Try me," he taunts, gazing across at me with lust in his eyes.

"Jaxon," I reply, biting my lip and swallowing hard, awaiting his reply.

"Bel! Really?"

"Yeah and it was damn good," I laugh reaching over to graze my hand over the growing bulge in his pants.

"Well, I guess I kinda get why you're confused. Are you sure you don't have feelings for him?"

"To be honest I don't know, but right now I want to feel and forget," I announce, sliding my hand into the waistband of his shorts and grabbing his cock through his boxers.

He lets out a verbal hiss, "Bel, fuck I'm trying to drive."

Smirking at him, I start rubbing my hand up and down his length. His cock grows in my hand and my desire starts to pool in my knickers.

I can tell he's trying to hold back from giving in to his impending climax and with one hand still on the steering wheel, he reaches back over to dive a finger into my wet folds again.

"God Bel, you're lucky I know this road like the back of my hand."

"Mmm, yeah and lucky it's straight," I tease, flipping his cock out of his shorts, still stroking it up and down as he plunges his fingers in and out of my wetness.

He glances over at me for a moment, as I plunge my other hand into my knickers, rubbing it over my clit.

"Mmm Bel, fuck you look hot touching yourself," he moans, tipping his head back slightly against the headrest as he tries to focus on watching the road ahead but also helping me ride the orgasm that ripples through me.

He pulls his finger out licking it clean, moaning.

My other hand is still stroking his cock and I can feel him beginning to shudder in my grasp.

Droplets of pre-cum are gathering on the tip as he shifts uncomfortably in the seat, gripping the steering with both hands like he's about to lose control.

"Bel, Bel, fuck!" He screams out as I lean over the gear knob, taking his cock into my mouth.

Bobbing up and down on his hard cock, I lick the pre-cum off the tip, running my tongue over it and up and down. He grips the steering wheel harder when his cock spasms in my mouth, his hot salty cum squirting down the back of my throat as his release takes over.

The Ute jerks forward, his foot pressing down on the accelerator when I swallow his load and remove my mouth from his cock.

"God Bella, you're something else."

"What do you mean?"

"You know exactly what I mean," he laughs smirking when he turns the Ute off the road into a secluded tree-lined parking area.

"Austin, why are we stopping here? It's only like half an hour til we get to Mum's."

He laughs, with a devilish smirk on his face as he cuts the engine. He strokes his cock to attention again, looking at me with eyes filled with lust.

"We're stopping here Bella because I'm fucking you right now, so take your soaked knickers off and climb onto my lap now," he demands.

His demand and the look in his eyes makes me feel giddy, not to mention turned on. Following his instruction I lift my arse off the seat a little and slide my knickers down my legs, kicking them and my thongs off.

He licks his lips as I awkwardly climb over the gear knob and centre console into his lap. Before he can even say a word I smash a kiss to his lips, teasing him with my tongue by running it slowly along his lips. It's oddly arousing tasting each others cum as we kiss.

Teasingly I begin to rock my wetness over his growing cock, making him moan as he continues to kiss me. Breathless he pulls back, "Bel, we don't have any you know..." he starts to say protection, when I kiss him again, sliding my body down onto his.

Pushing down all the way I stop a moment, loving having him rock hard inside me. He bites my lip as he kisses me harder.

I'm moaning, wanting so much more from him. Again I wonder if i'm lying to myself.

He breaks the kiss,"Bel? Are you sure?" He gasps huskily.

"Mmm, Aust," I moan, rocking my hips as I take him as far inside me as possible.

Leaning back as the pleasure overtakes us, my back crashes into the steering wheel, making the horn to sound repeatedly as we both moan.

"Mmm, Bel, god I love fucking you," he screams out as I bob up and down on him more, taking him so deep I scream out, "Austin, fuck, fuck!" as another climax takes over, even more intense than the one before.

He kisses me again hard and zealously, before asking, "Bel, can I cream inside you?"

I nod as I slow the rocking of my hips, the aftershock of my release sending shivers through my body as I feel the warm spurt of his release fill me.

"God Bella, why is the sex between us so damn good?" He asks as I climb back over to the passenger seat.

Laughing I reply, "Maybe because we're not in love."

"Maybe, but are you sure you don't have feelings for me?"

"Trust me Austin, I don't."

He smiles at me, putting his cock back into his pants as he starts the engine again.

"Thanks for the hot car sex Bel," he teases, "guess I better get you home."

I laugh when a thought pops into my head, "I had to pay you somehow for driving me."

"Oh really?"

"Yeah and hands down its been a much better trip than taking the bus," I laugh as we head back out onto the highway.

He laughs but doesn't reply, as though he's lost for words. We drive in silence for the next half hour and I try to tell my head to stop thinking, to stop wondering why I can have hot sex with Austin and not have feelings for him, but at the same time have hot sex with Jaxon and be so confused by how I feel about him I go running.

It feels like only minutes have passed when Austin pulls into my Mum's driveway.

"Are you sure you just want me to drop you off?"

"Yeah, I'll just grab my bag out of the back," I reply, my hand on the door handle opening it slowly.

"Ok," he smiles, "let me know if you want me to pick you up later. I'm going home for a couple of days too."

"Ok Austin, thanks. I'll text you later," I reply sliding out, grabbing my thongs and slipping them on my feet.

I'm about to grab my knickers when he shakes his head at me.

I laugh, "Austin, you're a dirty boy."

"Yep," he laughs, "bye Bella."

"Bye Austin," I reply, shutting the door and grabbing my bag out as I look towards the front window to see my little sister peeking out of the corner of the blinds.

Austin reverses down the driveway and I wave to him as I walk under the porch to be greeted by Elyse opening the door excitedly.

Twelve | Tastes like lust

Reversing out of the Mishall's driveway, I stop to watch Bella being strangled into a hug by her younger sister before I drive off.

I haven't told my Mum I'm coming home and can't wait to surprise her by turning up in twenty minutes. My mind is still a mess, as I'm still desperately in love with Anni, but I also can't stop thinking about Bella.

Granted all I want from Bella is sex and all that is between us is lust. At least it sure tastes like lust. Coming home at Christmas had been cringe-worthy as Mum had known something was up with me, but she didn't mention anything.

I hate lying to her and feel guilty for not speaking to her but I'm afraid I'll blurt out things mothers shouldn't know about their sons.

She always has a way of getting me to talk, even when I don't want to share with her. I love her, and always will be a bit of a mummy's boy but it's so damn annoying how well she knows me and can sense things even when we're apart.

Turning into the driveway of my childhood home, sounding the horn I glance around noticing that my Dad's car is missing from the carport.

I exhale a breath, that I didn't even know I was holding in, glad that I don't have to face him before talking to Mum.
As I cut the engine, the front door squeaks open.
Mum steps outside and looks straight at me, a wide smile crossing her face.
Racing over, she pulls me into a hug the moment I step out of the ute.

"Austin, son, what are you doing here dearest?"
Pulling back from her hug, I laugh, "Well, hello to you to Mum."
"Sorry dear, I'm just surprised that's all."
"I know, I should have told you I was coming home."
"Nonsense Austin," she laughs, as I grab my bag out of the back of the ute.

Following her inside she's speaking frantically, "Your Dad's not home, he won't be back until next week, some crazy business trip and Lillie is out at her study group."

"Mum, slow down," I break in, touching her arm to calm her down, "I'm here for a couple of days if that's ok?"

She opens the door ushering me inside. It makes me feel a little off, like I'm not her son but some uninvited guest.

Glancing around the house, it's a little unkempt, not the usual immaculately clean place it had been when I was growing up. Something just seems off, especially after my conversation with Lillie the night before.

Mum goes into the kitchen, as I head down the hallway to put my bag in my old bedroom. Nothing has changed since I left home, and it's comforting as well as concerning.

Throwing my bag on the bed, I sigh before heading back out to Mum in the kitchen. She doesn't look up when I enter, leaning on the square island bench in the middle as she makes a coffee.

"Mum, is everything ok?"

"Yes, dear, everything is fine. Would you like a coffee?"

"Yeah, thanks Mum," I reply, touching her arm lightly again.

She squirms a little, "Are you sure you're ok?"

"Austin, I'm fine. It's just that your Dad has been away a lot and Lillie is being a bit of a pain in the behind."

"I'm sorry Mum. I wish I could help."

"You don't have to Austin. You have your own life in the city now."

"Yeah, about that," I grunt, taking the coffee she hands to me.

"What dear?" she asks with that knowing tone, like she's digging it out of me.

"I don't know where to start Mum," I confess, sipping the coffee.

Starting to walk towards the lounge room, she asks as I follow, "Would it have something to do with Annika?"

Clutching my coffee, I sit in the recliner as Mum sits on the three seater next to me, putting her coffee down on the side table.

"Um, it...um," I mumble, sipping the coffee again, not able to meet Mum's eyes.

I'm about to tell my Mum intimate details about my love life. It feels kinda odd to talk to her about things like that.

"Austin, I know you're in love with her. You have been for years."

Putting my coffee down next to hers, I swallow hard before I reply, "Yeah, but it took me too long to realise how I felt about her and now I've lost her completely."

She lifts her coffee to her lips, taking a long sip as she considers her reply.

"How have you lost her completely dear?"

"The guy that came with us at Christmas is her boyfriend. They moved out together when we got back in January and I haven't seen or spoken to her since."

"Oh Austin, dear I'm so sorry."

"It's my fault Mum. I just always thought she'd be in my life."

"I know dear, but sometimes things don't turn out how we plan or how we think they should."

"Yeah, and it makes me as confused as hell."

"How so dear?'

"Well, I um..."

"Austin, don't hide anything from me. I know you've made some bad choices and I'm not blind to the fact that your not my innocent little boy anymore."

"I'm....um... I'm trying to block out how I feel about Anni by sleeping with someone else," I admit, feeling a blush rise up my cheeks that I just admitted I was having sex to my Mum.

"Austin Maxmillian Belvinz! That is a horrible thing to do!"

"I know Mum, but she feels the same about me. It's just sex between us, nothing more."

"Austin! It's never just sex!"

I shake my head at her, "Oh trust me, Mum, it is. Tastes like lust, not love."

"You need to be careful son. Who is this girl you're sleeping with?"

I feel the blush colour my cheeks again when I reply, "Bella."

"Bella Mishall?"

"Yes, I dropped her at her Mum's tonight. She's really confused about some stuff that happened with her ex-boyfriend and just wanted some time at home."

"Oh Austin, no! You can't get involved with Bella. That poor girl hasn't had the best life and I...I"

I slurp down the rest of my coffee.

"I don't want to be with Bella Mum, but what would it matter if I did?"

"I...just don't think she's the right girl for you."

I laugh at her motherly concern, "I know that Mum. I'm not going to fall in love with Bella. It's just a bad case of lust."

"Fine Austin, but please be careful with your heart dear. Heartbreak is hard to deal with once, let alone more than once."

"I know Mum. Thanks for the chat."

"No worries sweet boy. I miss you a lot."

Standing up I kiss her forehead, "I miss you to Mum. I'm going to head to bed, but I'll see you in the morning and help you get things back on track here."

"Thanks, son, I'd appreciate that. Could you maybe have a word to your sister too?"

"Sure Mum. Goodnight," I reply smiling as I pick up my coffee cup to take it to the kitchen.

As I put it in the dishwasher I hear a shriek from behind me, as two small arms embrace me from behind.

"Austin!" my little sister squeals, squeezing me so hard my breath catches in my chest.

"Lil, you're suffocating me!"

Pulling back, she squeaks, "Sorry Austy, I'm just so excited to see you."

"Yeah, I wanted to surprise you."

"Well, I'm flabbergasted Austy."

"Nice word Lil."

"How long are you staying?"

"Just a day or two," I yawn with a hand over my mouth.

"Yay! I've gotta go have a shower, but tomorrow we can chat yeah?"

"Yes Lil, we need to have a little talk," I jeer playfully tickling her in the ribs and stomach.

She giggles as she squirms, racing down the hallway to the bathroom. I follow, heading to my room instead. Grabbing my bag, unzipping it I grab out my sleep shorts and strip from my clothes as I slide them over my nakedness.

Sliding under the sheets, about to jack off thinking about old times in this very bed with Anni, I hear a pounding on the door and Lillie asking, "Austy, can I come in?"

"Lil, in the morning yeah?"

"I need to talk to you now," she begs, pushing the door open and peering in.

"Fine, what's up Lil?" I ask as she walks in and I sit up in bed, pulling the sheets up to my chin.

Sitting on the edge of the bed, she looks at me grinning, "El just text me saying that Bella is home and you dropped her off."

"Yeah, I did. Why has that made you so excited Lil?"

"Are you with Bella now? Is she your girlfriend?"

"No Lil, she's not ok. Things are complicated ok. You wouldn't understand."

"Are you not in love with Anni anymore?"

"Yeah, nah, I'm still in love with Anni, but she's with Jairus now."

"Is he the hot guy that came with you guys at Christmas?"

"Yes he is and..."

"God, she's so lucky," she giggles, "so are you going to get with Bella now?"

"No Lil I'm not ok. Just drop it yeah."

"Fine," she laughs, jumping up from the bed, "Goodnight big bro!"

As she leaves closing the door behind her, I close my eyes hoping to drift into a dreamless sleep. Love is a complicated emotion, but lust is just as complicated and my conversation with Mum is really bugging me. It makes me kind of feel like I'm destined to be alone forever, nursing a broken heart and trying to mend it with meaningless sex.

Thirteen | Don't tell Fibs

Bella

Sitting down at my Mum's kitchen table, I slowly spoon the soggy Fruit Loops into my mouth.

It's been forever since I've eaten breakfast cereal, let alone the sugary goodness of Fruit Loops.

Savouring each spoonful, not concentrating on anything else I nearly jump out of my chair when Elyse sits across from me.

"Morning Bel-bear!" She choruses, a little too chirpy for the early hour.

I'm not usually up at seven am, but I've not been able to sleep very well lately. My mind is still focusing on thinking about my time with Jax and his near confession of being in love with me.

Then there's Austin, who I know I not in love with but there is definitely lust between us that is hard to deny.

Sleeping with both them is not my best move, but the sex with Jax is undoubtedly some of the best I've ever had and it sends my mind spinning about whether there could be more between us.

Even when I was with Jace I'd always been closer to Jaxon as a friend and often confided in him about things brother's probably shouldn't know.

Now sitting at the table with my younger sister I wonder how much is too much to tell her.

"Morning Ely-bug," I greet her smiling.

I laugh at her taking a huge bite out of her Vegemite smothered toast.

She scoffs at me, "Don't call me that baby name Bel-bear."

"No fair Ely-bug, you're calling me Bel-bear."

"Ok true," she laughs, shoving the final piece of her toast into her mouth and loudly chewing it before continuing to speak, "so Bel-bear tell me why you came home and with Austin?"

"I can't tell you, Ely. You're too innocent to know."

"Am not Bella!" She snaps at me, scowling.

"Elyse...it's to do with sex."

She blushes, turning her gaze down as she swallows hard. Her mouth opens and shuts like she wants to say something but is afraid.

"Bel...I...um...I," she stammers, her blush increasing.

Standing up from the table with my bowl, I touch her shoulder whispering in her ear, "Let me put these in

the dishwasher and we'll chat in your room in case
Mum gets up."

She stands up, following me with her plate before we
head to her bedroom.

She sits down on the bed and I wrap an arm around
her shoulder.

"So Ely-bug are you trying to tell me you lost your v-
card?"

Tears fall down her cheeks as she looks up at me,
"Yes Bel, to Zack and it was horrible."

"Oh Ely-bug, why didn't you tell me?"

"Because I thought you'd be angry. I haven't even
told Mum and..."

"And what Ely?"

"The condom broke," she confesses biting her lip.

"Elyse no! Your not are you?"

"No I took the pill thing, but Zack didn't want
anything to do with me after."

I pull her closer, hugging her tight as I kiss her hair,
"Oh Ely-bug I'm so sorry, but you deserve better than
Zack Rudenstine. You're too good for him."

"But Bel I really like him and I feel like he used me."

"I know Ely, but most girls don't end up with the guy
they lose their v-card to."

"Yeah I guess you're right," she replies, sniffing back her tears, "who did you lose yours too?"

Laughing I reply, "Zach's older brother."

She laughs, "Really, you lost yours to Matt Rudenstine?"

"Yeah I know," I laugh.

We sit in silence for a moment, looking at each other smiling.

"So Bel-bear, are you and Austin together now?"

"No what gave you that idea?"

Again she blushes, moving back on the bed a little.

"I text Lil last night and she said that Austin was really suspicious about things between you."

"Well, um..."

"Bel-bear! Have you had sex with him?"

I feel myself blush this time.

"Yes, Ely-bug I have," I confess.

"So he is your boyfriend?" She jeers, poking me.

"No, he's not Ely. He's still madly in love with Anni, but she's got a new boyfriend who is sex on legs."

"Oh, do you want Austin to be your boyfriend?"

"God no Ely. It's complicated ok?"

She nods, "ok, so who is Anni's boyfriend? Do you have a pic of him?"

"No, but I can show you his Insta. He's a footballer for Richmond."

Her mouth gapes open, "What? That could only mean it's one of two eligible bachelors..." she muses, pressing a finger to her forehead as she thinks.

My little sister has always been into things like football, a girly tomboy as such and she knew pretty much all of the players under the age of thirty in the Australian football league.

"What are you thinking Ely-bug?"

"Are you telling me she's actually with Jairus Brooks for real now? He kissed her on the Brownlow red carpet last year."

I nod, "Yeah, she's lucky huh?"

"God, I'm so jelly! He's so damn hot!"

I laugh, "Like I said, sex on legs."

She licks her lips before asking, "So Bel-bear, if you're not with Austin do you have another boyfriend?"

"No Ely-bug, I don't," I reply hoping my cheeks aren't betraying me as thoughts of Jaxon crash into my mind.

"Don't tell fibs, Bel-bear!" she laughs, "You're blushing!"

"I'm not telling fibs Ely-bug. I don't have a boyfriend. I'm just really confused."

"Yeah, guys are so complicated."

"Yeah, I know," I laugh.

"Bel-bear?"

"Yeah Ely-bug?"

"Do you have to leave?"

"Yeah, I've got work on the weekend."

"Oh, um ok."

I smile at her, "How about I ask Mum if you can come to stay with me for a few days?"

She stands up, jumping up and down eagerly, "Oh yes Bel-bear! I'd love that."

"I can see that. Let's go ask her."

A few minutes later, with an eager Elyse following me I find Mum making breakfast in the kitchen.

I step up to hug her from behind, inhaling her perfume that is unmistakably her scent.

I miss her so much sometimes it hurts. Things hadn't always been easy, with her struggle with alcohol after Dad's death. But since being in alcoholic's anonymous and meeting her boyfriend Morris she'd been sober for nearly a year.

"Morning Mum."

She turns around to face me, hugging me tighter before kissing my forehead, "Aww good morning Bella beautiful."

I laugh at her silly nickname for me, "You know my name means beautiful Mum?"

"I know baby, but you're more beautiful than your name implies."

"Ok, Mum stop the soppiness. I have a favour to ask?"

"Ask away baby," she coos happily.

"Can Elyse come to the city with me for a few days?"

Mum frowns, looking at Elyse then back at me.

"I don't think that's a good idea, Bella. She has school."

I turn to look at Elyse, giving her a help me look.

"Mum please!" she begs, "I'd only miss a couple of days. I could come home on Sunday night."

My crazy little sister claps her hands together begging, "Please Mummy!"

Again Mum looks between us both, before she replies, "Fine, you can go Elyse, but you will take my emergency credit card."

Elyse launches herself at Mum, hugging her screaming, "Thank you, thank you, Mum!"

"Ely-bug, calm down girl," I laugh.

Mum touches my arm lightly, "Bella you're not to use any of your own money on anything Elyse needs. Do you understand?"

"Yes, Mum," I reply, kissing her cheek.

Elyse grins before running back down the hallway.

Mum turns back to stirring her porridge on the stove,

"Mum, are you sure its ok?"

"Yes, it's fine Bella. I actually wouldn't mind some time alone with Morris," she replies blushing.

"Are things getting serious with you guys then?"

"Yes, baby. I haven't felt anything like he makes me feel since your father."

"That's really great Mum. I'm glad you're happy," I reply, hoping she doesn't sense that I'm not feeling the same happiness myself.

"Bella, is something wrong? Did you fight with Austin?"

"Um, no...Austin and I aren't together Mum."

"But he dropped you off the other day?"

"Yeah, but we're just roommates...friends I guess," I reply hanging my head low when I feel that I'm blushing.

"Just friends or something else baby?"

"We um..."

"Bella, be careful baby. Sex always leads to feelings."

"Yeah, I know Mum. I'm really confused."

"About how you feel about Austin?"

"No, someone else."

"Baby girl, you cannot go around sleeping with so many different guys."

She turns the stove off and puts her hands on my shoulders.

"Bella, I've never told you this, because you look so much like me, but um..."

"What Mum?"

"Your father isn't actually your father."

She tries to pull me into a hug but I step back, "What the fuck Mum? How could you not tell me something like that?"

"I didn't want to upset you. He was your father in every way that mattered and asked me to marry him even though I'd slept with someone else and gotten pregnant with you. It was a mistake, one night when we'd had a massive fight."

"So do you know who my father is then?"

"Yes, but he didn't want to know anything about you. I lost contact with him years ago."

"I...I can't believe this Mum. I can't be here another minute. I'll send Elyse home on the Sunday night train."

I don't let her say another word before I storm out of the kitchen slamming Elyse's bedroom door behind me.

"We are leaving now. Get some other clothes on."

"What happened Bel-bear?"

"I cant talk about it. Just meet me outside in fifteen minutes and get Mum's credit card before you leave. It's going to get a workout."

"Um ok Bel-bear," she replies meekly as I leave the room.

Back in my room, I grab my bag slinging it over my shoulder before running out the back door.

The anger is rising in my chest, my breathing fast, my heart pounding.

Pushing through the gate I take a deep breath to calm myself when Elyse walks out the front door.

"Ready Ely-bug?"

"Definitely ready. I'm so excited. Lillie will be so jelly!"

I laugh, "I bet."

Taking my little sisters hand we run down the road together towards the train station. At least with her around for a few days, I'll be able to think with my head and heart, instead of giving into lust.

Fourteen | Close off emotions

Again I find myself at boxing, feeling pent up with emotions and lust I have nowhere to let out.

Bella is still at her Mum's and I'd come home after I hadn't heard a response from her about getting a lift back.

It has only been a couple of days since we'd been together, fucking in my Ute on the way to Ararat but I want to be with her again.

When I can't lose myself in the mindless sex my mind drifts to thoughts of Anni and it makes me miss her like hell.

Kaden steps up behind me in the change rooms, a little to close as our bodies almost brush against each other when I turn around from shoving my clothes in my locker.

"What's with you mate?" He asks, running a hand through his unruly blonde hair.

"Nothing," I snap stepping aside as I put on my gloves, "why you doggin me?"

He laughs, throwing his head back as he looks at me weirdly, "Because you're in the fucking dumps about something and I'm sick of being around ya sorry ass."

Not replying I walk out to the punching bags, hitting one hard and cursing when I feel the jolt right through my glove.

Kaden steps up to the bag next to me, not taking a punch, but instead staring at me like he's waiting for a reply.

I meet his gaze, replying shakily, "I'm confused mate. okay?"

"What about? Bella?"

"Nah...well yeah kinda," I reply shaking my head.

He turns to face me, again making me feel uncomfortable.

"Tell me about it man. Get it off ya mind."

I take another hit of the bag, trying to shake the uncomfortable feeling.

"Fine! I miss Anni so bad my heart literally feels like its breaking. But..." I confess before cutting my own words off, not even sure of what else I want to say.

"But what?"

Sighing I reply, "It's not the physical of being with her I miss. It's everything else."

"What do ya mean?" Kaden asks, confusion plastered on his face.

"I told her everything...everything. I miss the little things we'd do together that weren't related to sex."

"Oh shit mate! I'm sorry, I didn't really think about that stuff, but this soppy missing her stuff is what's getting you down."

"I know, I know but I can't help it. You know feelings get to me."

"Yeah, you're a fucking pansy sometimes but you gotta shut them out if you're ever going to move on."

"Easier said than done mate," I suggest, feeling stupid for even saying the words.

"True true," he replies before asking, "but what about when you're with Bella?"

"I'm just thinking about how good the sex is to be honest."

"Really? Wasn't the sex with Anni any good?"

"Oh no it was better than good with Anni. It's just not the same as sex with Anni was. It takes the edge off and scratches the itch so to speak but that's it."

"Ok, so you can't see it being more than just sex with her?"

"Fuck no Kad!" I snap a little too quick. He looks like I've slapped him.

"Why mate? She's hot," He laughs.

"Yeah but it's not just about that Kad...you know that."

"Yeah I know...we need to get you out of this funk bad," he suggests taking a punch of his bag.

I laugh, feeling a sense of relief at getting my feelings off my chest, "How about pizza, beers and video games after practice?"

"Yeah i'd be up for that."

"Sweet, did you tram it today?"

"Yeah, two months left until I get my licence back."

"You're an idiot Kad."

"I know, but so are you," he jeers playfully slapping my arm with his glove.

"Oh no you didn't, its on mate!" I jeer back turning towards him and putting my gloves up to say c'mon at me.

He puts his up, hitting mine as we start to square off against each other. He reaches down to punch my abs, but I slide aside so he misses. The look in his eyes confuses me somewhat and for a moment I wonder if he's hiding something from me.

It seems possible but impossible at the same time.

Laughing I put my hands up in the air, "ok, ok, truce. Let's head out. I'm starving."

"Yeah me to mate," he replies firstly licking his lips before he pats me on the back as we head to the change rooms.

Maybe I'm not wrong.

Fifteen | Exposure so scandalous

Kaden

Awkwardly, as I try to still hold my PlayStation controller, I grab another piece of pizza from the box on Austin's coffee table. Scoffing it I gulp it down hard, before laughing at Austin cursing at the game as I catch him off guard by appearing around the corner of a building ready to shoot his character dead.

"Kad! How are you so fucking good at this game?"

"Practice my man, practice!"

"You're killing me, I'm the video games major and you're whipping my arse," he yells, frantically pressing the buttons on his controller to make his character flee.

I gulp again, his words 'whipping my arse' are still in my mind and I don't have a coherent response to say. My body wants to press pause on the game to whip his arse for real.

Thoughts of being with him had been plaguing my mind for a while, but I know he's not bi and I can't afford to lose my closest friend just because I want to kiss him among other things.

Shaking the thoughts from my head I try to focus on the screen, looking at Austin out of the corner of my eye every so often.

Only a few minutes pass when he curses again, his controller vibrating in his hands as his character falls to the ground dying.

He throws his controller on the couch next to him, "Well I'm done. I'm getting another beer. You want one?"

I look up at him as he stands up from the couch. Stretching his arms above his head lifts the hem of his white t-shirt up and I again swallow a gulp, finding my voice coming out a little husky, "Ah, yeah thanks mate."

He walks off to the fridge and I watch his arse shift in his tight jeans.

Thinking about grabbing it in my hands I press the wrong button on the controller and the game over screen flashes on the television as Austin returns with a beer in each hand.

"Fuck I hate this game," he laughs sitting back down next to me, handing me a beer.

I scull a bit before I reply, "Yeah, the war games are all the same."

"Yeah, I was thinking of creating a Zombie war game for my final coding project."

"Sounds awesome. Are the zombies gonna fight the humans?"

"Some shit like that," he laughs grabbing another piece of pizza.

Watching him eat it, I shift uncomfortably on the couch when a drop of pizza sauce collects on the corner of his mouth and his tongue darts out to lick it away.

"You ok Kad?" he asks shoving the crust into his mouth and chewing it quickly.

As I find words to reply, I try to not look at his Adam's apple bobbing as he swallows.

I shouldn't be feeling this attraction to him, but I've been kidding myself for months that I don't find him hot as hell.

"Yeah yeah, I'm fine. Just thinking."

"What about? Have you got girl troubles too?" he jeers touching my arm, sending a shiver through me.

"Um...no," I snap, my heart pounding when he looks at me with a questioning glint in his eyes.

"Um ok...hey I forgot to ask you how your date went a few weeks ago? Did she put out?"

Fuck, now what Kaden....you can't lie to him, can you?

"Not she Aust," I acknowledge, looking across at him to see my words sink in.

"Um...sorry what?"

"My date wasn't with a girl," I confess.

His eyes boggle for a moment, "So are you telling me you bat for the other team?"

"No Austin I'm not gay."

"But?"

I laugh, calming myself by running my hands through my hair, "I'm bisexual Austin and until recently I haven't acted on my attraction to any guy."

"So um...did you...did you on this date?"

"Yeah, but I don't think you really want to hear about it."

"Um no not really," he replies biting his lip and blushing a little which gets me a little too excited.

"Was it good with him? Are you sure you're actually a Switch hitter?"

"Yes Aust it was really good...and yes I'm sure," I reply before downing the rest of my beer.

He laughs hard, pressing a hand against his stomach,
"So anyone you've got your eye on? Are you gonna
see him again?"
"No...because I think another guy is hot...and I..."

*Don't Kaden, don't tell him you are getting a stiffy
from talking about sex with him, get a hold of
yourself*

"Who Kad? Do I know him? Is it John?"
I shake my head, looking straight at him when I lick
my lips again.
Tentatively I reach over, placing my hand on his thigh.
His eyes lock on mine, but he doesn't move an inch
or smack my hand away.
My mind is racing, telling me to do it, to take the
chance and kiss him.

Sixteen | Pashing Caught Out

Kaden's eyes are locked on mine, his hand on my
thigh gently squeezing it. His palm is clammy giving
me the sense he's nervous about something.

His confession didn't shock me; the thoughts from
earlier in the day flashing again in my mind.

His lips part again; his mouth slightly agape for a
moment before he licks his lips again as his hand
slides up and down my thigh.

"Aust...um...I...want.."

It might be because I'm horny as fuck but his hand on
my thigh is oddly arousing.

"What Kad?" I ask, swallowing a lump in my throat as
I wonder if I want what I'm pretty sure he wants.

"Aust," he purrs my name, "can I kiss you?"

He shifts on the couch so he's facing me.

Again I swallow hard, not replying but nodding and
preparing myself for his lips on mine.

I don't have much time to overthink about the fact
I'm about to kiss a guy as he smashes his lips to mine,
hard. It's a simple kiss, his lips against mine for barely

a minute when he pulls back as though I've done something wrong.

"I'm sorry Austin. I...um...I've wanted to kiss you since I met you, but you're obviously...oh fuck it," he mumbles standing up from the couch.

He's looking at me still like he wants to say something else and isn't sure if he should stay or go.

My mind is racing, wanting to kiss him back.

Tentatively I stand up, as close to him as he'd been earlier when I felt something was weird.

"Kad?"

"Yeah?" He murmurs, stepping back a little.

"Kiss me again like you mean it."

"Austin, are you sure?"

I laugh instead of replying and close my eyes as I kiss him back. This time he moans before making the kiss fierce by opening his mouth; smiling against my lips.

His kiss is hard, hot and zealous; rawer than kissing a girl.

His tongue runs along my lips, forcing my lips to part.

I can't deny that it's turning me on, especially when he bites my bottom lip, wetting it with his tongue as he pulls back on it before his lips completely devour mine.

I have no idea what to do with my hands, so wait a moment to follow his lead.

As his hands push up the hem of my t-shirt, his touch makes my breath hitch so much I break the kiss breathless.

"Fuck Kad! That was hot as," I murmur.

"You have no idea Austin."

He's wrong that I have no idea about how kissing him makes him feel; it's plainly obvious in the front of his jeans.

"You're a little turned on Kad," I laugh.

He blushes, "I like you Austin ok? I seriously never thought I'd actually get to kiss you, like ever."

"Yeah well, I never thought I'd kiss a guy, let alone like kissing a guy."

His blush deepens when he asks, "You weren't repulsed?"

"Far from it Kaden," I inform him grabbing the hem of his shirt as I step back, my knees crashing against the couch.

"Austin, please," he drawls, "please don't tease me."

"I'm not. I don't know why but I want to pash you so bad right now."

"God, you seriously have no idea how long I've wanted to hear you say that," he growls pushing me down on the couch and climbing on top of me.

He slides his hand up under my t-shirt, pushing the fabric up, exposing my abs. His hands slide up my sides and instinctively I lift my arms above my head. With an arm on either side of my body, he leans in against my chest, kissing me zealously like he can't get enough. His hard cock is pressing against my stomach, sending a peculiar rush through my body as he continues kissing me.

"Mmm Austin, god...I..." he moans, about to reach down between our bodies when I hear a voice in the room.

"Bel-bear," the voice calls out, "why are there guys pashing on your couch?"

Kaden sits bolt upright, quicker than I can push him away. He doesn't even look at me as he stands up, "Aust...um...I gotta go. I'll see you at practice."

I'm completely tongue-tied, not moving from the couch as I watch him walk out the door brushing past Bella as she enters the lounge room.

Standing now in my lounge room is Elyse, Bella's younger sister and my little sister's best friend.
I feel the blush rise up my cheeks from what she's just caught me doing.

"Hey Elyse," I greet her.
"Um hi, Austin. Who was that hottie you were pashing?"
"No one," I snap standing up and grabbing Bella's arm to drag her away from her little sister's earshot.

In her ear, I whisper, "Why didn't you tell me you were coming home?"
She pushes me away as though she's annoyed.
"I don't have to tell you everything Austin. Clearly, you don't tell me everything."
Scuffing my feet on the floor, unable to meet her eyes I reply, "Well um...it just happened."
"Sure Austin. You looked like you were pretty close."
"As friends yes, but he um..."
"What? Just came out of the closet to you?"
I laugh as her words are kinda true.
Elyse is standing next to us, texting on her phone but obviously listening to our conversation.
"No, not exactly. He confessed that he's bi and I was curious."

"Oh ok, bi right."

"And he also thinks you're hot Bel."

Her eyes boggle, as though she's thinking the same dirty thought I am.

"Oh no Austin! Don't go there!" she jeers punching my arm before leading Elyse towards her bedroom.

I can't help it, my cock is straining against my jeans as my mind has already gone there; straight to the gutter.

Seventeen | So That Happened

After barely sleeping a wink, having been thinking about my hot as fuck pash session with my guy best friend and how much I want to watch Bella kiss him as well I get up early to grab some breakfast.

Being a Thursday I have the day off and before pashing Kaden, I'd planned to head to boxing to get some extra training in but I'm not sure if I can face him.

Kissing him had been so good, so good it turned me on and had my mind racing all night.

Questions plague my mind, questions I've never ever thought I'd face asking myself.

My body's reaction to Kaden's kiss surely means something about my sexuality. I've had crushes on guy's before, but doesn't everyone have those?

I've never felt any type of attraction to a guy before to the point that I got a hard-on thinking about them. With Kaden's kiss replaying in my mind, my cock, much to my surprise rises a little in my pants.

There is no way I can face him yet, without

confronting my own feelings.

My feelings are so mixed up though, still in love with

Anni, lusting after Bella and now thinking about if I

want more with Kaden.

Like I'd told Kaden though I miss Anni

desperately and now I want nothing more than to

talk to her, confide in her about how I feel but I can't.

It's breaking my fucking heart over and over again.

In the kitchen I open the cupboard, searching for

something quick to gulp down for breakfast.

The large open box of Fruit Loops is screaming at me.

Grabbing it out, I find that only the last broken

remnants are in the bottom of the plastic inside in

the box.

Leaning against the sink I lift the box to my lips,

tipping the contents into my mouth, chewing the

sweet glory before swallowing it hard.

About to put the box down I hear her voice as she

comes into the kitchen, "God Austin, you're a fucking

pig."

Putting the box on the bench I laugh, "Good morning

Bel. How'd you sleep?"

"Fine, although I um..."

"What? I taunt stepping towards her, grinning cheekily.

"I was um thinking about..."

"Really Bel?"

"Yes," she replies huskily, looking towards my crotch and the tent that has risen in my daks.

Pushing my body against hers I press my cock against her body and whisper in her ear teasingly, "So you're up for a threesome Bella?"

Her chest rises as I kiss her neck, teasing her more as I trail kisses down her neck, up her chin before licking her lips and taking her mouth in a hard fierce kiss.

She moans wrapping her arms around my neck and fisting my hair in the way she knows that drives me crazy.

Against my lips, she murmurs, "Aust...I..."

I pull back, resting my forehead against hers, my lips only a centimetre from hers when I ask, "Is that a yes, Bella?"

"Mmm..." she moans, closing the distance between us by kissing me again.

My confusion level hits the roof, as kissing Bella is so damn arousing but so is kissing Kaden.

Wanting to take things further with Bella as usual, still kissing her I push her body against the kitchen bench.

Hoisting her up to sit on the edge I kiss her harder,
my fingers gathering the hem of the night tee that
lays across her thighs.

Again she moans against my lips as I start to lift the
night tee further, up her torso.

It's at her breasts when a shocked voice screams out
from the other side of the kitchen, "Bel-bear! What
the fuck?"

Bella jumps down from the bench, brushing against
my aching cock as she steps aside. Her cheeks flush a
deep shade of crimson as she looks at her younger
sister who's innocence has been tainted several
times over since she's set foot in our house.

Elyse has not moved, instead she's standing in the
middle of the kitchen, her hands on her hips with an
angry look on her face.

Bella crosses the room towards her, pleading, "Its...
it's not what it looks like Ely-bug."

"Really? Really Bel-bear? Not what it looks like?"

'No...it's um...well you know what I told you."

"Yeah I do, but Bel-bear you were...you were...in the
kitchen," Elyse spits at her older sister, scoffing after
like she's confused.

"I know Ely-bug, ok? I'm sorry you had to see that."

"Yeah me too," Elyse laughs, looking across at me.

I'm leaning against the bench trying not to laugh.

Elyse steps up to me, invading my personal space.

"You better sort out how you feel about my sister,

Austin!" she jeers at me, poking fingers into my abs.

Putting my hands up in mock surrender I reply, "Ok

ok, Elyse! I promise I will! Pinky swear?"

I hold my pinky finger up to her and she links it with

hers, "Pinky swear, Austin Belvinz," she taunts

giggling when she continues speaking, "and you bet

I'll be telling Lillie."

"No Ely please, please don't say anything to my sister.

She already has the wrong idea."

"Well, I can see why. Just make it official already," she

suggests, looking at me before turning to Bella with a

pleading look.

"Ely-bug, just drop it ok," Bella says to her in a slightly

chastising tone.

"Fine," Elyse snaps in a huff.

"How about you get dressed and we head out to give

Mum's credit card that workout?"

"Oh yes!" Elyse squeals, "I'm going to shop til I drop!"

She gives Bella an eager hug before she races back

down the hallway towards the bedroom.

Bella turns her gaze back to me, "So that happened

huh?"

I laugh, "Yeah and I'm sorry Bel. I'm so fucking confused right now."

"Yeah? Was kissing a guy hot for you?"

I feel my cheeks darken, "Yeah it was actually and I fantasised last night about watching him kiss you while I...well you know." I gesture jerking off with my fist.

"Fuck Austin, you're a dirty boy," she teases, winking at me.

"Only when it comes to you Bella," I tease back, smirking.

She licks her lips, "Sort out how you feel, but ask that hot as friend of yours if he's up for it."

"You think Kaden is hot?"

She steps closer to me again, standing on her tiptoes to purr in my ear, "You weren't the only one who fantasised last night Austin."

Grabbing her cheeks in my palms I smash a kiss to her lips, "Mmm Bel, hearing you say that turns me on so bad."

She laughs so sexily my cock aches, "Watching you kiss another guy turned me on, Aust."

"Bel," I moan, "You need to get out of this house right now or I'm going to fuck you here right now," I taunt pressing my hand against the bench.

"If only Elyse wasn't here," she teases as she leaves the room.

Even though my feelings are mixed up, I know that I want to be with both of them.

It would at least block out any thoughts of Anni, if only for a little while.

Eighteen | Talking about Elephants

Kaden

Austin had been avoiding me since our hot pash session on his couch a few days earlier. It had been the only thing on my mind, the thoughts of going further with him being my go to wank material. If we'd not been interrupted, my hand would have been down into his daks to jerk him off as I ravaged his mouth.

I've always known I'm bi, even though I've never been with a guy until more recently. Feeling attracted to both girls and guys is just normal for me, but until meeting Austin a couple of years ago I'd never actually felt as though I liked a guy enough to want to be in a relationship with them.

Of course, I had to fall for a straight guy, although after kissing him and his odd reaction I wonder if I'm losing my mind, that maybe he's bisexual as well.

His avoidance of me is making me crazy, all I want to do is talk to him about our kiss, but I know for him it's going to be the elephant in the room. He'd told me himself that feelings get to him big time and I'm sure he is feeling a mix of emotions, as am I.

Seeing Bella again has also messed with my head a bit, she was just as gorgeous as the first time I'd seen her at Austin's house party last year. I like Austin, but I'm definitely attracted to Bella in a purely physical sense.

My arm brushing past hers as I made my hasty exit sent a delightful shiver through me.

If it wasn't for the seemingly innocent younger lookalike of hers that caught Austin and I out, I'd have suggested we head straight to the bedroom to explore the attraction between us all. Having a threesome is something that has always intrigued me.

It's often something I watch porn of, and it makes me both turned on and horrified at the way the girl is always treated as an object.

If I ever get the chance, I'd want to make it all about pleasure, for the girl and the guy if he was down for that.

As I get changed, ready to go hard at boxing I hear my phone ping in my gym bag. Grabbing it out, a smile spreads across my face seeing a message from Austin.

Aust: Kad, mate are you at boxing?

It's stupid to be smiling at him still using my nickname and calling me mate, but it makes me happy as though our kiss hasn't made him completely cut me out of his life.

Kad: Yeah, missing ya. Where you at?
Aust: Needed a break. Be there in twenty. We need to talk

And there it is, those four words that no one ever wants to hear, the elephant in the room.

~~

Almost exactly twenty minutes later, as I'm punching the bags harder than I usually would Austin saunters into the arena like a man on a mission.

His fiery red hair is sticking up everywhere, held back off his forehead with a bandana. He's wearing trackie daks low on his waist and a singlet top that dips low down across his abs.

He looks even more gorgeous than usual and my cock is straining against the front of my shorts.

Seeing me, he harshly grabs my arm, pulling me away into the change rooms. Having him be so harsh turns me on so bad. The moment we enter the change rooms I quickly check the surroundings for others, before smashing his body against the lockers, standing right in front of him with a hand on either side of his body, pressing them into the lockers to steady myself.

Smashing a kiss to his lips, I moan deeply when he doesn't protest again.

Starting to deepen the kiss though, he whimpers turning his face from mine and pushing his hands into my chest to make me take a step back.

"Kad, please don't. We need to talk," he pants, pressing his palms into the locker behind him. He lets out a shaky breath, calming himself.

"I'm sorry Aust. I...god you look good."

"Kaden..." he says my full name illicitly like he's saying it during sex.

"Austin," I drawl his full name, swallowing the lump in my throat, "I fucking like you so much and after our kiss the other day and just now I can tell you feel something for me too."

He smashes a fist against the locker behind him, "I don't know what I feel Kad, ok? I'm fucking confused!"

"I know, but?"

"There is no but Kaden. I like kissing you and it scares the fucking shit out of me. I feel like I'm losing my fucking mind."

"You're not Aust."

"Sure fucking feels like it. This," he gestures towards me with a finger, "this us, it, can't be."

It's my turn to get a little riled up, "Why the fuck not Austin? I like you! I want to be with you!"

"Yeah I get that Kaden, but this whole being attracted to a guy is new to me."

"I know, but it's not for me. So why not explore it more together?"

"Because I'm not gay Kaden," he spits at me.

"Neither am I Austin."

"Arggh, you know what I mean."

"Yeah I do." I smile at him.

"Kaden, can I ask you something? You can say no?"

"Yeah, sure I guess. Sounds like a proposition?"

He laughs, blushing, "Well it kinda is."

"Oh really? You asking me out?" I jeer, winking at him.

"No...I'm...I'm wondering if you'd be up for a threesome?"

My mouth gapes open, his words hit me hard as though he's read my mind.

"Fuck, yeah!" I scream, possibly a little to eagerly, "Are you sure though? And with who?"

"I'm sure. I've been thinking about it for days."

I laugh, "Yeah me too, but who with?"

"Bella," he announces biting down on his lip.

"Is she up for it?"

"Yeah, she actually told me to ask you."

"Well, I'm definitely down. Is her mini-me still around?"

"Yeah, that's her younger sister Elyse. She heads home tomorrow."

"Oh right cool. She was feisty, kinda hot too."

He laughs at me, "Seriously Kad! Is there anyone you're not attracted to?"

"Yeah, so maybe next Thursday or Friday?"

"I'll ask Bel and text you."

"Ripper," I reply, turning towards my locker to pack up for the day.

Even after our conversation, there still feels like there's an elephant in the room.

I feel Austin walk around the benches in the middle of the room and know he is right behind me when he speaks, "Kad, have you ever had a threesome?"

Turning to face him I reply, "No, but it's always been a fantasy of mine."

"Yeah me too, but with two girls though, well until now that is."

"It will be hot Aust, I know it will be."

"Yeah, with Bella I don't doubt it will be."

"She's a wildcat in bed huh?"

"You have no idea," he laughs with a delicious smirk on his face.

He has no idea how gorgeous he is when he smiles.

All I want to do is pash him, touching him all over until he comes apart but it isn't the time.

The end of the next week can't come quick enough, as I'm more than ready to have my hands and lips all over him and the equally gorgeous Bella.

Nineteen | Ring on it

Annika

The last couple of months since I'd moved in with Jairus had been nothing short of amazing. Every time we are together is super hot and he never lets me forget how much he loves me.

He's also showered me with gifts, chocolates and sexy lingerie, never telling me though how much money he actually earns in his football career, or how much he's spent on all the gifts he given me.

I've never watched so much football in my life and I was actually finding I enjoyed learning the in's and out's of our countries great game.

Of course, it helps that my man looks as hot as hell in his tight footy shorts. Watching him play my mind often wanders to when we get home and I pull them down his toned legs before we'd end up having sex somewhere in our penthouse.

He'd told me he wanted to fuck me in every room and on every surface; in the last couple of months, we'd done just that many times over.

He's at an early training session now and I have a day off from Uni so I'm pottering around the house enjoying a leisurely breakfast with a glass of iced coffee.

Making my porridge I can't help but stare at the sparkle of the ring on my left hand.

It still hasn't sunk in that I'm engaged, to Jairus Brooks, to one of the hottest eligible bachelors in the Australian football league.

Many hearts were shattered when he proposed to me on the weekend during the medal presentation of the Pre-season grand final.

It was so perfect and I'm still floating on cloud nine.

The only people I've told so far are my parents who were absolutely ecstatic, my Mum nearly screaming my ear off down the phone.

Sitting at the dining table scrolling through Instagram I decide I should probably tell Bella, partly because I can't hold my excitement in much longer and I want to post a picture of my gorgeous ring on Instagram.

I really want to tell Austin too, but knowing he's still in love with me, hearing of my engagement to someone else is likely to send him over the edge.

Quickly with one thumb, as I spoon porridge into my mouth, I type a text to Bella.

Anni: Can we catch up again, for lunch?

Bel: Yeah I guess, late lunch? I finish work at 2

Anni: Ok...can I meet you at work

Bel: Yeah ok cool. is everything ok?

Anni: Yeah of course. Just have to tell you something.

in person

Bel: ok see you soon

Excitedly I finish my porridge, downing the rest of my
iced coffee, before skipping to the ensuite to get
ready.

Putting simple makeup on, I smile at my appearance
in the mirror.

At times I still can't understand how a guy as
gorgeous as Jairus finds me so attractive, but he
constantly tells me the fact I don't know how
beautiful I am; is what makes me so beautiful to him.

The weather is still quite warm, even in early March
so I choose to wear a blue and white stripy sundress.

Slipping thongs on my feet at the door I grab my
handbag, making sure my swipe card is in the pocket
where I always keep it.

In the elevator, leaning against the rail I think about
every time I get in the elevator with Jairus. He always
kisses me when we get in and I laugh thinking of the
afternoon an elderly stepped in on a lower floor.

She looked us up and down, flushing as she looked at Jairus, and smiling at me like she was saying, you lucky girl.

Reaching the parking garage I contemplate not taking my car into the city, but considering where Bella works I'll be able to scam free parking so I jump in my Beemer, cranking my music up as I drive out of the parking garage.

~~

Walking into Lush, the smell of all the bath products is overwhelming. Bella sees me as I come in, rushing out the back to grab her stuff. She waves to her colleagues and follows me out.

"Gloria Jeans?" she asks.

"Up to you," I reply as we step onto the escalator.

"I'm easy," she coos, "but totally starving."

"How about TGI Fridays? I could smash down those chicken tenders right now."

"Sounds good," she replies, her tone a little odd.

Stopping at TGI Fridays, we wait for a table. Bella isn't saying much and I'm a little worried.

Once at our seats I quiz her, "Bel, are you ok?"

"Well, um, yeah, nah," she mumbles not able to meet my eyes.

"Bel, please talk to me."

"I'm confused, Anni."

"What about? Did something change with you and Austin?"

"Not exactly. I um...I.."

"Tell me, Bel, please."

"I slept with Jax and it was really good, like really good and he nearly confessed he was in love with me."

"Woah Bel! Do you think you have feelings for him too? Is that why you're confused?"

"Yeah, and things with Austin have been complicated. Sometimes my feelings from high school come crashing back."

"What? What feelings from high school?" I snap, completely shocked at her sudden confession.

"I had a mega crush on Austin before he got with you."

"How come you never told me, Bel?"

"I thought you'd be mad, that I'd try to steal him from you."

"Oh Bel, I'm sorry," I reply when the waitress comes over to take our orders.

Quickly we both order the chicken tenders and large choc-mint milkshakes.

"Don't be Anni. I've gotta sort out my feelings and stop sleeping around."

I laugh, "Yeah, you're a naughty girl Bella."

She laughs then before asking, "So what did you need to tell me?"

I hold out my left hand, grinning as her eyes focus on my ring.

"Oh my God Anni! Really?"

"Yep! On the weekend, at the pre-season grand final. Travis called me up on the stage and Jairus proposed. It was so sweet."

"Wow Anni, that sounds amazing. I'm so jelly! And this ring, fuck!"

"You have no idea! Apparently, it cost him a month's salary and we both know how much that is for Jai."

Her eyes boggle as my words sink in, "Well it's beautiful Anni. I'm so happy for you girl! Naturally, I'm hoping to get Maid of honour duties."

"Of course!"

Our food arrives, and Bella takes a couple of bites before she asks meekly, "Are you going to tell Austin?"

"I...don't know. He'll be heartbroken Bel."

"Yeah, I know. Maybe leave it for now. He's confused enough as it is."

I give her an incredulous look, "About what?"

"Well obviously, he's still in love with you but he's really confused about something else."

"What? His feelings for you?"

"No," she laughs taking a sip of her milkshake before continuing, "his sexuality."

I nearly spit my food out. "What? What do you mean?"

"I caught him kissing a guy on the couch the other day."

"Oh my god Bel! What? I...I can't believe it."

"Yeah, I was shocked, but he's really confused about how he feels now."

"I bet," I laugh, taking a big slurp of my milkshake.

We eat in silence then and I think about Austin. I miss my best friend so much it hurts. I want to tell him I'm engaged, but with this new found information I don't want to make things worse.

Taking the last bite of my food, I laugh wondering what Jairus will say when I tell him Austin might be batting for the other team.

After our plates are cleared, I pay for us both and ask Bella as we walk out, "Do you want a lift home?"

"Nah, it's all good. I need to do a couple of things before I head home."

"Ok, are you sure?"

"Yeah, I am. Congrats again Anni. I'm so happy for you," she says, hugging me.

"Thanks, Bel. Please don't tell Austin."

"I won't Anni," she replies sheepishly, "I'll see you soon."

She walks off, waving at me until I can no longer see her. I take the lift to my car, again cranking the music up as I drive home to try and block out the thoughts of my once best friend and the pain of not being a part of his life anymore.

Twenty | Scorching Counter Playtime

Jairus

Getting home from a killer all day training sesh, all I want is to see Anni. We've barely seen each other in the past few weeks, as she headed back to Uni and I've been in the thick of the pre-season.

The only way I've gotten through the past few weeks was thinking about making love to her in every room of our penthouse. The night of proposing to her on the weekend was the last time we'd slept together and it had only been a couple of days but I ache for her.

She isn't home now, so I strip my footy clothes off throwing them in the laundry basket hearing her in my head telling me to 'not be a dirty boy'. I love the innocence she still has sometimes.

Pulling on my tartan pyjama pants I head out to the kitchen to make a coffee and call her.

Sitting on the breakfast bar stool I dial her number, sipping on coffee whilst I wait for her to answer.

"Hey baby," her voice comes down the line into my ear.

"Hi, sweetheart, where you at?"

"Just coming home from the city. I caught up with Bel."

"Ok cool, how far are you?"

"Turning into our carpark now," she replies.

"Ok sweetheart, love you," I say into the phone as it cuts out.

Slurping down the rest of my coffee, I watch the door for her to come inside. The whole house is silent, so I hear the click of the door as she touches her swipe card against it.

Walking in she smiles at me, licking her lips as she saunters into the kitchen kicking her thongs off.

She stops in front of me, running her hands over my bare abs.

"Hey baby, I missed you," she purrs.

Her touch warms my skin, sending a rush through me that only she can.

"Mmm, sweetheart I love your hands on me," I murmur, as she runs her palm teasingly over the front of my pyjama pants.

The touch is light but it makes my cock rise to attention.

"Looks like you missed me baby," she teases, grabbing my cock in her fist.

"Mmm, you bet I did sweetheart," I tease back, wrapping an arm around her waist to pull her closer. Opening my legs wide she steps in between them before kissing me.

Kissing her fiercely my hands run all over her, edging up the back of her dress as I grab her arse in my palms, squeezing the soft flesh to tease her.

She is wearing cheeky knickers that barely cover any skin and feeling my hands on her she whimpers in pleasure against my lips, before breaking the kiss and holding her arms above her head to invite me to strip her of the dress.

Grabbing the hem that grazes the top of her thighs, I gather it up, lifting it over her head and throwing it on the floor.

"Mmm, sweetheart you take my breath away," I murmur, looking over her exquisite body in a longing gaze.

She leans in, kissing below my ear before she teases, "Take me right here, right now, baby."

Touching a hand against the kitchen counter behind me I lock my eyes on hers, "Right here, right now on this counter sweetheart?"

"Yes," she hisses, kissing me hard again.

Still kissing her I stand up from the bar stool, my hands brushing over her sides before I make quick work of plunging her cheeky knickers to the floor.

Moaning as she continues kissing me, smiling against my lips, her fingers slip into the elastic of my pyjama pants and she makes quick work of dakking me.

She giggles, breaking the kiss when she realises I'm naked.

"Do you see what you do to me, sweetheart?"

She doesn't reply, instead reaches around her back to unclasp her lacy bra, her eyes not leaving mine for a second.

"Oh Annika, you're so fucking beautiful," I roar grabbing her around the waist.

Jumping into my arms, she kisses me as I turn around so her arse is on the edge of the bench.

 Breaking the kiss I run a finger down her body, stopping at the sensitive bud that makes her hips arch up from the jolt of pleasure that pulses through her.

"Lie back sweetheart," I instruct her.

She follows my words, not replying, letting out a hiss at the feeling of the cold stone against her back.

Running a hand down her body, I palm her breasts making them rise to attention.

"Stay still sweetheart," I tell her, running my palm down to her wet core, brushing a finger over her clit before pushing it inside. Her hips buck against my hand and she moans, "Oh Jai, fuck."

I laugh, growling as I bend down and bury my face in between her legs.

Slowly I lick her, my tongue darting in and out of her dripping slit, over her clit. She can't stop the elicit moans of pleasure escaping her lips, saying my name over and over again as her body climbs the peak.

With a final flick of my tongue against her bud, her climax rushes through her, a moan so carnal leaving her lips it makes my cock harder still, pulsating with the need to be inside her.

Standing up I look at her smirking, "Mmm, sweetheart, I love making you cum."

Smirking back without saying a word, she grabs the silver chain around my neck, hooking it in a finger to pull me down for a sweet kiss.

My aching cock teases her, the tip just at her entrance.

"Jai, baby, please, I want you."

Kissing her again, a little harder, I glide inside her. Her hips rise to meet mine, pushing me deeper as I fuck her fiercely. Moans of pleasure escape her lips, driving my desire for her higher as we both head towards our climaxes.

Grabbing her hands I place her arms above her head, holding them there as I kiss her, my tongue fucking her mouth, my cock fucking her body with reckless abandonment. Every time we have sex I feel as though I'll never get enough of her, the feeling of being with her is absolutely pure ecstasy.

Breaking the kiss, after a lascivious moan against my lips, she asks, "Jai, touch me?"

"Mmm, yes," I growl, reaching down between our bodies to touch her bud, pounding into her harder again to hit the spot deep inside that makes her writhe beneath me in sheer pleasure.

"Mmm, Jai, fuck, oh...baby, fuck," she pants as I thrust into her, harder and deeper than ever, our bodies completely one.

"Come for me sweetheart," I order her, "I want to watch you come apart with my cock buried inside you."

"Mmm, Jai...baby...fuck...I" she screams out, her whole body twitching as she rides the wave of her release.

"God, Annika, fuck sweetheart!" I scream out, my own release exploding into her as I thrust into her one last time.

Smiling at me, she pulls me down to her lips again for a quick kiss, "That was scorching baby," she says as I pull out of her body and wrap my arms around her waist so she stands up, our bodies still pressed against each other.

"Mmm, sweetheart it was flaming hot, just like you."
Laughing she replies, "Yep devastatingly hot like you baby."

"I love you, Annika," I declare kissing her forehead, wrapping her into my embrace tighter.

"I love you too Jairus."

We're both silent for a moment when she pulls back from my embrace with an odd smile on her face.

"What sweetheart?" I ask, wondering why she's about to break into a fit of giggles.

"Bel told me that she caught Austin pashing a guy."
I look at her as we step apart, not sure if I've heard her words right. "So he's gay now?"
Laughing she replies, "I don't know about gay but yeah maybe I guess."

"Well, I guess I don't have to worry about him stealing my girl now do I?"

"You didn't have to worry about that anyway baby. When I fell in love with you, there will never be anyone else, forever."

"Oh Annika, you have me forever to sweetheart. I didn't know what love meant until I met you."

"And what amazing sex was too," she laughs, walking away wiggling her hips seductively.

"Oh really, amazing sex huh?"

"Yep, amazing, mindblowing sex," she drawls out stopping by the dining table, leaning against it with a devious smirk on her face.

"I might just have to lay you back on the table then for some more of that amazing mindblowing sex," I tease as I walk across the room towards her.

My cock is already hard again, just thinking about having her again.

"Yes please baby," she teases as I grab her around the waist, smashing my lips to hers for a heart-shattering kiss.

Annika is mine, forever and I can't wait until I can call her my wife. There isn't much else I want in my life, except maybe the chance to be a Father.

I can only dream, and with the amount of sex we have that my dream might be just around the corner.

Twenty-One | Feelings Suck Balls

Bella

Knocking on his door, part of me hopes he isn't home. I've not seen him nor text him since our week of hot sex all over his apartment.

About to walk away, the door swings open and he's standing against it shirtless, with jeans low on his hips.

"Bel, what are you doing here?"

"I...um need to talk to someone."

"I don't think coming to me is a good idea, Bel."

"Please Jax, just let me in. I don't know who else to talk to."

"Fine," he snaps, stepping back from the door to usher me inside.

Crossing his small apartment, we stand awkwardly in his lounge room, the silence between us deafening. Opening my mouth like a carp, I try to speak but close it again just as quick as I opened it.

"So Bel, are you going to talk to me or not?" he asks.

"Well, I um...I don't even know where to start. I'm really confused."

"About what?"

"How I feel,"I declare with a huff.

"You'll have to be more specific Bel."

"About Austin, about you...after we...."

"About me huh?" he taunts, brushing the hair from my cheek as he takes a step closer to me, the couch grazing his knees.

Before I can think of another word to say in reply, he breaches any space left between us by kissing me. My mind feels fuzzy, even more confused with Jax kissing me as though he can't get enough.

Pulling back his words shock me a little, "Bel I'm sorry about last time we were together. I shouldn't have said, well you know."

"Don't Jax... I'm not ready to face my feelings, feelings suck balls."

He laughs deeply, "Bel don't say that."

"Why?" I ask in a suggestive tone.

"It puts visuals in my head and makes my cock hard," he laughs again, nodding towards the front of his jeans.

Smiling I reply, "Jax I don't think we should."

"Damn it, Bel, you're such a fucking tease...you've barely left my mind and now you come over not having talked to me for months and you won't even suck me."

"I'm sorry Jax," I apologise, biting down on my lip.

"Don't be fucking sorry Bella...just suck my cock, please," he begs, locking his eyes on mine in a silent plea.

Grabbing his cock I taunt, "Is that what you want?

"Yes Bella," he hisses, "I want your mouth around my cock."

Undoing his belt and ripping the button down fly open I dak him.

Pushing him down on the couch I kneel in front of him.

"God Bel, you on your knees is so fucking hot," he growls, flipping his hard cock out of his boxers.

Grabbing it again, I run my hands up and down watching the lustful look in his eyes.

Bending over him I take his length into my mouth, licking from his balls all the way to the tip, swirling my tongue in teasing strokes.

"Mmm, Bel, fuck that feels good," he moans, fisting my hair and pushing me down harder, his cock grazing the back of my throat.

I continue licking the tip, droplets of pre-cum tingling my taste buds before I pull back looking up at him.

"Bel? Come on, you can't..." I cut off his words, taking his balls in my mouth to suck and lick them, biting the soft flesh between my teeth.

"Fuck, Bel, fuck!" he screams out as I continue the delicious torture on his balls whilst stroking a hand up and down his cock.

Harshly he pulls me back by the hair, "Please Bella, take me deep now. I want to cum in your sweet mouth."

Again I slide my lips over his cock, teasing the tip again with my tongue. I move my head up and down in a steady rhythm, preparing to milk his climax from him.

"Oh fuck Bella, I love you" he screams out, his cock spasming in my mouth as he shoots a shot of warm salty cum into my mouth.

Swallowing hard I slide my mouth off his cock, wiping an arm across my face as stand up, not able to meet his eyes.

Embarrassment hits me, I feel like a complete idiot and his words make panic rise in my chest.

"No, you don't Jax. You can't love me," I stammer, grabbing my handbag from beside me on the floor.

Turning away, I rush towards the door sensing he's behind me but I don't dare turn back to look at him. Instead, I leave, slamming the front door behind me and running to the tram.

I'm angry at myself, angry for my stupidity, for letting the lust take over again.

So many feelings are swirling around in my head, none of them actually for Jaxon.

Feelings might have made me suck balls but now I realise I have feelings for no one, not Jaxon and definitely not Austin.

Twenty-Two | Hitting The Grog

It's strange going out on a Friday night
again. Thoughts of going out with Anni the last time
tumble in my mind and I find myself glancing around
Rivera as though she's going to be there.
I'd almost protested with Kaden, asking if we could
go somewhere else but by the time we'd gotten
inside it was well past ten pm. He paid the cover
charge for me, so I can't exactly drag his arse
elsewhere.
He grabs my hand as we enter the club, dragging me
up towards the bar.
"You're not buying me a drink as well Kad."
"It's fine Aust, I want to. So what ya having? Beer or
something harder?" His tone is a little suggestive and
I find my gaze lowering to the front of his dark jeans.
"Beer to start," I reply licking my lips and swallowing,
my mouth that feels oddly dry.
"Coopers or James squire?" he asks.
"Coopers."
"Nice, a man after my own heart," he replies winking
at me and signalling the barman.

He orders the beers, the barman quickly sliding them towards us as Kaden hands over the cash to pay for them.

Taking a sip, a lick of foam collects at the corner of Kaden's lips. His tongue darts out to lick it and I sigh deeply watching him.

I'm still feeling an odd attraction to him and I've been researching threesomes for a week, trying to set my own boundaries.

Some of the stuff I'd watched looked utterly pleasurable and some downright fucking painful, for all parties involved.

"Aust, why are you looking at me like you're about to pash me?"

"Oh um...no reason. You um...just had some foam on your lips."

He laughs, a deep jovial belly laugh that makes my insides stir.

"Did I get it off?"

"Um yeah you did."

"Damn, I thought I was going to get a pash."

"Yeah um," I mutter, gulping and taking a quick sip of my beer to not say something I'll regret.

Kaden laughs again, cuing the odd butterfly sensation in my stomach. I'm acting like a god damn girl, feeling all giddy with attraction for him.

"So you're going to pick up tonight, forget about Anni and even Bella for the moment until next week."

"Yeah I guess," I reply reluctantly, looking at him over the rim of my glass as I gulp down more of my beer.

"You gotta lighten up Aust. Look around at all the hot bodies in here, drinking, dancing like nobodies watching."

"It just it makes me think of Anni, that's all."

"Why?"

"The last time I was here, we danced and pashed all night on the dance floor," I say looking down at my feet. He's pushing me to open up, to face my feelings and it's making me panic.

He locks his gaze on mine, expectantly,"Did something else happen? I would've gone somewhere else man if I knew."

"It's ok, it was just she dry humped Jairus on the dance floor too right in front of my fucking eyes."

"Shit man, that sucks."

"Yeah, so how about we get a harder drink and dance like idiots?"

"Sounds like a plan. I like the sound of something harder," he replies again with the same suggestive tone.

I quickly lose track of how many drinks I've downed and even in my drunken state, I know I look like a right idiot dancing with Kaden.

The song changes to an old classic and a girl lets out an excited screech dragging the guy she's been sitting in a booth with towards the dance floor.

My eyes lock on hers in the darkness and the recollection hits me. It's the same pretty brunette I'd bumped into outside the lecture theatre a few months ago.

Leaning into Kad's side I whisper yell into his ear, "I saw her at Uni a few weeks ago and know her from somewhere else but can't place her." I point towards her, watching as lust pulses through my friend.

He literally can't contain his excitement, whenever a brunette girl is in sight.

"Damn, she's hot Aust. Have you been with her another night maybe?"

"No nothing like that," I reply shaking my head, "she just seems really familiar."

When the song changes to something slower, Kaden laughs as he walks back towards the bar for another drink. The brunette starts dancing with the guy and I try to focus on him, realising who it is when he spins her away and back again.

Kaden comes back over, sliding into a booth after
handing me another beer.

"Kad I know where I know her from."

"Where man?" he asks, sipping on his beer.

"She's in the cheer squad for Richmond."

"Oh right.

I stand up to go and speak to her but notice she's
kissing him now.

For some odd reason, my heart sinks and I head to
the bathroom to drain my snake.

When I return, sliding back into the booth Kaden
asks, "Why didn't you go dance with her?"

"She's taken, man."

"By who?"

"Jairus' best friend...I don't know his name," I say,
Anni's boyfriend's name like poison on my tongue.

"Oh, shit...well find another sheila then. You can take
your pick I'm sure."

"Just forget it, Kaden, ok?"

"You've got to move on though man," he says in a
different tone like he really does care.

"Yeah I know, but right now I don't think I'm ready
yet."

"Fair enough let's just get tanked then."

"I think we're drunk enough Kad. Maybe we should
call it a night."

He looks at me with lust in his eyes, "Yeah, ok."

Standing up I start walking out with Kaden on my tail.

"Aust slow down, what's the hurry?"

"Kad please, I just want to get home."

"Fuck Aust, anyone would think you're a cock tease. You've been suggestive all night, giving me the promise in your words of heading home for the night and then run out so fast. You confuse me so fucking much."

"I'm sorry Kad ok? I'm just so fucking confused. I've been thinking about the threesome and also about..."

"About what Aust?"

"This," I say pushing him against the wall and kissing him hard.

He moans against my lips, deepening the kiss with a bite on my lower lip.

Breaking the kiss a few moments later, he huskily says, "God Aust, I want to do so much more than kiss you."

"Not yet Kad."

He laughs, "I seriously can't fucking wait and hearing you tell me you've researched things is such a fucking turn on."

It's my turn to laugh, "It was eye-opening and admittedly a turn on."

"Mmm, yeah. Are you sure I can't convince you to head back to mine?"

I bite down on my lip, "I um...don't know Kad."

He puts his hand against his heart, "I promise just kissing unless you want more."

I kiss him again, answering him with my lips before I pull away and hail a taxi.

He gives the driver his address, his only words before his lips are back on mine as we drive to his Hawthorn apartment.

His kiss is turning me on so much and my mind wanders a little to thinking of what else we could do other than kissing.

Twenty-Three | Undressing Naked Fantasies

Kaden

Packing up my bag from getting an extra boxing session in, my phone pings in my bag.
Grabbing it out I find a text from Austin lighting up my screen.

Austin: can't wait to get dirty with you and bel

Touching my lips thinking about our night together a few days earlier my cock already starts to strain against the front of my tight grey bonds jocks.
I've barely stopped thinking about kissing him senseless and taking his cock in my mouth until he explodes. He still keeps denying that he's bi, that he has any feelings for me but his actions and the fact that he always gets turned on around me says otherwise.
Quickly I tap a reply.

Kaden: me too Aust. anything you're not up for?

His reply is quick.

Austin: anything but arse play Kad

I send him a smiley face emoji before throwing my
phone in my bag.

Quickly I dress, slipping my navy Nike trackies on
before adding my white tank.

Obviously, I don't plan on wearing it long once I get
to Austin's house.

As I leave the boxing studio my mind wanders to not
only getting naked with Austin again but also seeing
the hot as Bella naked.

I'd watched her dancing at Austin's party, grinding
her sweet curvy arse against Annika.

It was an odd night for me, as not only had wicked
thoughts of Bella tantalised me but watching Austin
staring at Annika with love and lust made me realise
how bad I want him to look at me like that.

I don't want to fall in love with him, he's practically
my best friend but being with him has definitely
brought my feelings to the forefront of my mind.

He isn't going to fall in love with me, as he's still so
hung up on Annika and quite possibly Bella.

It doesn't stop me from wanting him and isn't going
to put a damper on enjoying the night with them
both.

Stepping up to the front door of their Richmond apartment, I swallow hard as I rap a hand against the door. I'm not sure if Austin or Bella is going to greet me.

My answer soon comes, when Bella opens the door leaning against it smirking at me as she looks me up and down.

She's wearing a silk cherry red baby doll that barely covers any skin.

Over her breasts, it has lace that her nipples are peeking through, they harden looking down at the bulge in my trackies.

"Hi Bella," I drawl, licking my lips, "You look fucking hot."

"Hi Kaden, so do you," she murmurs, ushering me inside and stepping a little closer to me.

Stretching up on her tiptoes she smashes a sudden hot kiss to my lips, making my cock harden instantly.

As Bella devours my mouth I hear Austin enter the room.

My lips are still locked with Bella's when he steps up behind her, brushing her hair aside to kiss her neck.

She moans against my mouth, breaking the kiss and tipping her head back in pleasure.

Austin continues kissing her neck, locking eyes with me as he reaches between Bella and I to grab my cock. I let out a hiss of pleasure looking between him and Bella as he palms my cock, making it ache with need.

"Aust, fuck..." I growl, eye fucking him as he teases Bella. He stops his torture on my cock, his hand sliding under the hem of Bella's baby doll.
His lips pucker as he leaves a hickey on her neck, "Kad," he moans grabbing my neck with his other hand and pulling my lips to his in a heated kiss.

Bella is still sandwiched between us, Austin is still teasing her by caressing her with a finger. His hand as he makes Bella shift in sweet moans of pleasure, is brushing against the front of my trackies and I just want to feel his skin against mine, as well as feel Bella's softness in comparision.

Breaking the kiss I step back looking Bella up and down, "God Aust, watching her is as hot as you said."
"I told you Kad," he laughs.
It's then I notice that he's shirtless, only wearing sleep shorts low on his waist exposing the delicious v of his muscles.

Bella stretches her neck back kissing Austin, again making my cock ache. I've never been so turned on in my life. I want them both so bad.

Breaking the kiss, she moans, "Bedroom, now..."
Nodding at Austin I laugh when he scoops her up in his arms, throwing her over his shoulder and slapping her bare arse.
He takes my hand, sending tingles through me as he leads me down the short hallway to Bella's room.
Throwing her down on the bed she moves back as we both stand by the bed looking at her.

She has an apprehensive look in her eyes, and turning to look at Austin I find he does too.

"Bella, tonight is all about you...whatever turns you on...whatever makes you moan in pleasure."
She bites down on her lip, "Mmm, I like the sound of that Kaden."

"So, tell me, Bella, what turns you on?"
She laughs, throwing her head back, flicking her luscious brown hair before she replies huskily,
"Watching you and Austin pashing."
"Mmm," I moan hearing the lust in her voice.

I'm just about to press my lips to Austin's when Bella's voice interrupts, her tone seductive, "I want you both naked while you pash."

"Mmm, gladly, "I laugh dakking Austin quickly in one swift movement, gaping when I see his cock is rock hard.

He winks at Bella before his gaze is on me and he's licking his lips.

His fingers brush the hem of my singlet lifting it up and over my head so quickly we barely break eye contact. Stepping closer to me he licks my lips, down over my Adam's apple and chest until he reaches the waistband of my trackies.

Everywhere his lips touch my skin feels hot, alive. His hands grab my hips, as his tongue slides down my own v muscle. I can barely think as his hands reach inside my trackies, grazing over the tent of my cock.

"Just do it," Bella laughs from the bed. Austin looks up at her, still torturing me with his hands, "Only if you do Bella."

She doesn't utter a word, instead lifts the baby doll over her head throwing it across the room.

My eyes gaze over her nakedness, taking in her small waist and perfectly rounded breasts.

She's a walking wet dream and I don't know what I want to do first, pash and play with Austin or dive at Bella to make her moan underneath me.

Austin suddenly daks me, both my trackies and jocks in one swift movement.

Bella's eyes lock on my cock, her tongue wetting her lips so seductively before she curses, "Fuck Kaden, your cock is...fuck!"

I laugh, teasing her, "I'd love your mouth on it later, but first..."

I turn my gaze back to Austin, stepping closer to him and kissing him harder than ever. He moans, I moan, feeling the skin of our cocks brushing against each other.

For a moment I forget anyone else is there until I hear the sweetest moan of pleasure, a low rumbling of the word 'Fuck' escaping Bella's lips.

Breaking my kiss with Austin, I turn to find Bella touching herself furiously.

"Bel, don't you dare cum," Austin taunts kneeling on the bed in front of her, before pulling me down beside him.

He looks at me, a question on the tip of his tongue as he opens and closes his mouth.

"What Aust?" I ask.

"Do you want to taste?"

"You know I do...but..."

"But what?" he asks, pulling Bella's hand out from beneath her legs.

He holds it up to my lips, Bella whimpers as I take her finger into my mouth licking it clean as my eyes dart between them.

"Fuck Bella, you taste damn good."

Austin dives a finger into Bella's folds, her hips buck up as he teases her and she whimpers, suddenly demanding, "Kaden, kiss me."

Leaning over her I smash my lips to hers, parting them with my tongue and loving the moans escaping her lips as Austin pleasures her.

Still kissing Bella, I feel Austin's hand grip my cock as he shifts on the bed. His hand strokes me and Bella breaks the kiss when Austin dives between her legs, his kiss tasting her and his tongue flicking against her clit.

"Mmm, Aust fuck, god," she screams out.

For a moment I just watch them together, enjoying the view of others in pleasure.

I almost can't believe my ears when Bella says,

"Kaden, I want to suck your cock."

I'm worried what Austin will think, but know he's okay with it when he releases my cock from his grasp.

Sliding up the bed, I put the tip of my cock between her lips and her tongue licks it teasingly in lavish strokes as she lets out sweet sexy moans.

The hot sucking noises she makes as she licks are enough to almost send me over the edge.

"Fuck!" I hiss as her mouth takes me in, fully.

Her soft lips feel so amazing, her tongue still circling over every nerve ending is pure ecstasy.

She's moaning as she takes me deeper, her hips writhing as Austin continues fucking her with his tongue.

I feel her teeth bite down on my cock as her climax hits, her body still riding the wave as I unload into her mouth, my cock spasming as she swallows every last drop.

I turn to look at Austin, his cock is still rock hard and he's licking Bella's juice from his lips.

Bella is still looking at us both with the same lustful look in her eyes, like she hasn't had near enough pleasure for one night.

"Aust, kiss me," I demand, "I wanna taste her on you."

I can't think when he smashes his lips to mine, pulling me closer so his cock is brushing against my stomach. I feel myself getting turned on again, but I want Austin to feel the same pleasure I did moments coming into Bella's delicious mouth.

Grabbing his rock hard cock in my grip I break the kiss.

"Aust, can I suck your cock?" I ask, hoping just like the other night he won't say no.

"Mmm, Kad please suck me now," he moans, making my own cock harden a little again.

Taking his cock into my mouth, I tease the tip, sliding him further down my throat than I previously have. The bed shifts and looking up as I swirl my tongue over Austin's cock I see Bella is behind him, reaching down his body and caressing his balls as I suck him.

He tips his head back, moaning in pleasure, "Fuck Kad, Bel, fuck." She kisses him then, biting his lips and taking his tongue with hers.

Grabbing my own cock, I fist it to attention as I suck Austin's cock harder and deeper whilst listening to their kiss and hot as hell moans.

Austin lets out a delicious growl, breaking his kiss with Bella, "Kad, fuck I'm gonna cum."

His cock pulses in my mouth, his warm salty milk coating the back of my throat before he pulls out and I swallow it down hard, licking my lips to taste the drop left behind.

My cock is again rock hard and Bella's staring down at it again, like she wants another taste. She looks towards Austin with an odd look in her eyes, something unspoken between them.

He nods and she locks eyes with me, "Kaden, I want you to fuck me."

"Mmm, Bella, I'd love to fuck you girl," I tease, giving her a kiss.

"Where do you want me?" she asks in an oddly innocent tone.

I tap the bed, "On all fours girl, and a franger?"

Crawling up the bed on fours she opens the drawer beside the bed, handing me a franger that I tear open, quickly sliding it onto my cock.

She arches her back towards me, her arse in the air, her words teasing, "Fuck me, Kaden."

Sliding into her wet folds from behind, slapping her curvy arse cheeks I push deep, balls deep when I feel Austin slide up behind me.

His cock is hard again and pressing against the top of my arse.

Pulling in and out of Bella as she moans in pleasure I want nothing more than to feel Austin slide between my arse cheeks and fuck me hard as I fuck Bella but when I shift a little to give him entrance he shrinks back.

Inwardly I curse myself, knowing he isn't ready. He'd clearly said no arse play so I have to play it cool, hoping the time for us to actually fuck is going to be soon.

Bella is pushing her arse back against me, keeping herself steady enough that I can reach behind my body to pull Austin closer to me.

Again his cock brushes against my arse as I rock in and out of Bella.

Bending my head back I kiss Austin, trailing kisses up his neck to nibble on his earlobe before I whisper, "I'm sorry Aust."

He gives me a soft kiss in response, "Aust, I can tell you it feels damn good."

"I trust you Kad," he whispers kissing me again as I thrust harder into Bella.

"Kaden, touch me please," she moans, looking up at me. Stopping my kiss with Austin I reach down, laying over Bella's back and teasing her clit with my thumb.

"Oh fuck Kaden, fuck!" she screams out as I thrust harder, my climax filling the latex inside her as her walls tighten around my cock, her climax rushing through her again, her whole body twitching as she milks my release.

As I pull out, she collapses on the bed, splaying her arms out beside her.
Austin lays down beside her as I get up to discard the franger in the bathroom.
They are kissing when I lay down beside them. My heart sinks a little, as it feels like I'm not there and that maybe they are both lying to each other about how they feel about each other.

Breaking the kiss Austin brushes a stray hair from her cheek, "You okay Bel?" he asks her softly.
"Better than okay, that was amazing. But Aust?"
"Yeah Bel?"
"You're still turned on bad."
"Yeah, but it's ok. Get some rest yeah?"
Smiling at him she closes her eyes and Austin looks at across at me.

"I'm sorry about earlier Kad. I...um...I"

Smiling at him I reply, "I get it Aust ok, but you trust me yeah?"

"Yeah, but Kad I'm confused. Really confused. I kinda want to have you fuck me, but god I don't know. Did you feel like this?"

"Yeah, of course. But you have to trust me. I like you Austin, a lot."

He doesn't say anything, just sits up the same time as I do. With Bella asleep between us he kisses me, less carnal than any kiss we've shared before, making my heart pound.

I've just lied to him and then he kisses me like he's feeling the same way. I pull away a little breathless.

"Aust, to be honest, I'm fucking in love with you."

Shock crosses his face and his response nearly breaks my heart, "No you aren't Kad. You can't be in love with someone who can't love you back."

I don't respond at first, instead lay back down next to Bella as he lays down next to her on the other side.

I want to leave, but it's well after midnight and I've forgotten my wallet so have no money for a taxi home.

I hear Austin's voice in the darkness, "Kad you can go and sleep in my room if you want?"

"I'm good," I snap back, closing my eyes and reliving the night in my head.

My fantasy has been fulfilled but I still want more from Austin. I should have kept my fucking mouth shut as I'm now afraid I'm going to lose him completely.

Twenty-Four | Dangerous After Shocks

Bella

Sometime during the early hours of the morning, I free myself from the boys embrace, in particular Austin's and head to the bathroom to piss.

After our hot as threesome when Kaden left the room to clean up Austin had pulled me close kissing me passionately, unlike any kiss we've shared. It was possessive and made my heart pound.

Feeling Kaden get back into the bed, I couldn't bear to look at him as I suddenly felt a rush of emotions hit me hard. Austin asked if I was okay and I wanted to say no but instead lied to him making sure he was ok before I drifted off to sleep.

As my mind drifted away I heard muffled sounds, the boys kissing, Kaden confessing he was in love with Austin. And it hit me then when Austin replied saying you can't love someone who doesn't love you back. His words were so far from true, because after a night with someone else in the bedroom with us and my recent escape from my feelings with Jaxon it's clear in my mind.

Standing at the sink in the bathroom, I splash water onto my face, cursing myself as I look at my face in the mirror.

Fuck Bella, you're in love with him.

I hate that my mind now knows what I've tried to keep from it, but since I'd sleep with Austin nearly a year ago I'd been falling for him.

All I've done is lie to myself, and try to push my feelings away by sleeping with Jaxon. Walking out of the bathroom I find the boys have entangled themselves together in their sleep.

For a moment I think about going to sleep in Austin's room, but I also want to doze for a bit longer and wake up in Austin's arms. We never cuddled after sex and we hadn't even had sex for weeks since he'd driven me home.

He's now on the side of the bed away from the wall, so I slide back into bed next to him, draping an arm over his chest. He murmurs and rolls over to face me. My body heats instantly, my heart hammering.

All my feelings have hit me head on. His lips are just a breath away from mine, his cock hard pressing against my entrance.

He inhales a long deep breath, almost scaring me when he speaks without opening his eyes, "Morning Bel."

"Morning Austin," I say, pressing my body against his.

He lets out a slight chuckle, "Seems like you're up for morning sex?"

"Mmm, yeah," I murmur closing the distance between us by kissing him softly.

He kisses me back, deepening the kiss in the same sweet possessive way he'd done the night before.

Again it makes my heart soar and I want to be closer to him, to be with him again, skin to skin.

Breaking the kiss he runs a hand down my cheek, "Bel, are you ok? That was some kiss."

"I'm fine," I mutter, pressing my aching crotch towards him.

"If you say so," he says, a slight smirk on the edge of his lips, "Were you jealous watching Kaden and I together?"

"No, but I..."

"What Bel?"

"Wanted to fuck you instead, but didn't want Kaden to get jealous. He seems to really like you, Aust." He laughs, the smirk on his face again when he replies, "He confessed he's in love with me."

Even though I know this news I reply with shock in my tone, "Oh shit Aust."

"I know, but I don't feel that way about him. I really like being with him, but I just can't see myself falling for a guy."

"Hmm yeah, but you can't help who you fall in love with Aust, you know that."

"Yeah," he chuckles softly, "So how about that morning sex?"

I kiss him again in reply and he wraps his arms around my waist as he slides inside me. Side by side we fuck, slowly rocking our pelvises together. It's more sensual than any other sex I've ever had and my heart feels like it's going to burst out of my chest. It isn't just sex to me, it isn't just fucking, this is the kind of sex you have with someone you're in love with.

"Mmm, Aust, fuck, I've...I..." I moan as he pushes into me harder.

Against my ear, I feel his breath when he whispers, "What Bel? You've never been fucked this way?" Looking him straight in the eyes, turning my head back to look at him, I reply, "No, I've never had sex like this, and god Aust, it's so fucking good."

"Mmm, Bel," he moans pulling all the way out before sliding back in.

It's delicious, hot dirty, naughty torture with Kaden lying next to Austin on the other side of the bed.

He moans, his arm draping over Austin.

Austin flinches, chuckling a little, lifting a finger to his lips to say 'shh'. His breath is at my ear again and he moans as he thrusts into me so deep I think I'm going to come apart right there and then in an intense rush.

His cock is brushing against my arse, "Bel, fuck, I'm gonna come so hard, Bel."

Kissing Austin, I reply against his lips, "Make me come, Aust, make me come so hard."

"Mmm, Bel, I love making you come," he moans as he drives into me one last time.

My climax hits me, rushing through me like a tidal wave and I can feel my body clenching around Austin's pulsating cock inside me as he releases his climax into me. With our bodies still together he kisses my forehead, "God Bel, that was amazing."

"Yeah, I um, I..." I'm about to confess my feelings, about to tell him I'm in love with him when I hear Kaden's voice, "Morning. Did I dream it or were you just fucking in the bed next to me?"

My face flushes deep crimson as Austin turns to look at Kaden next to me, "You weren't dreaming man. And you grinding your cock against my arse, fuck man."

"Sorry, morning wood. You know how it is."

"Yeah," Austin replies laughing and looking at me with an odd look in his eyes that makes me wonder about his feelings after the sweetest dirtiest sex we've had together.

"So do you usually wake up and fuck each other? Or was it just because of our hot as night together?" Kaden asks, not directing the question to either Austin or me.

Austin replies before I can even open my mouth, "No Kad, we don't usually have morning sex, but Bel and I didn't fuck last night, so well, you know."

"Hmm, yeah sure, Aust. I think there's more to it than that."

"There's not Kad," he replies, slapping his friend's chest.

"I don't believe you Austin. You two need to own up to your feelings for each other," Kaden replies sitting up against the wall with the sheets thankfully covering his cock.

Austin sits up next to me then, looking Kaden straight in the eyes, "I don't have feelings for Bella, Kad, you know that!"

His voice is harsh and it hurts when he looks at me apologetically.

"Could have fooled me Austin! I might have to get with Bella's hot little sister so you two can be together because I obviously don't have a chance with either one of you."

His words shock me, I want to scream at him for everything that happened the night before, for pushing his way into our lives. He would not get near my little sister with his ten-inch cock, not now, not ever.

I jump out of bed, ready to hurl abuse at him, but the words freeze on my tongue and I run into the bathroom to hurl the contents of my stomach into the toilet.

I don't know how much time passes, how long I'm sitting on the cold tiles of the bathroom clutching the toilet bowl.

The door creaks open and a fully clothed Austin enters the room. I look up at him, still hugging the porcelain of the toilet bowl when he asks, "Bel you ok?"

"Does it look like I'm ok?" I snap trying to stand but I feel weak and dizzy. The whole room feels like it's spinning.

Unsteadily I wobble on my feet, falling into Austin's arms.

"Bel, is this just about what Kaden said or is something else wrong? Did you throw up?"

"Is he gone?" I ask, looking up at Austin's face and melting into his arms that pull me closer when he replies.

"Yes, he's gone. Bel, did you throw up?"

"Yes," I hiss, stepping back as the realisation hits me.

"Bel! No! Please tell me you're not?"

I shake my head, "I don't know Aust."

"Fuck, not again!" he curses, taking a step back from me and running his hands through his hair before he rushes out the bathroom without another word or second glance at me.

My heart shatters. My whole world is falling apart
and I have no idea what I'm going to do.
Having a threesome might have felt good in the
moment, but it has brought up some dangerous
aftershocks.

Twenty-Five | Take my number

Since Anni had moved out, Bella and I had struggled with the rent on our apartment.

I didn't want to have to find another roommate, as it hadn't exactly worked out in my favour before but it was inevitable.

This time I decided to advertise by putting an ad up on the noticeboard at Uni for a new roommate.

At the bottom, I printed the little tear-off strips with my phone number on them.

Pinning it up, I rip the little strips apart before I step back sighing, hoping someone will notice the ad soon.

Being on Centrelink payments is barely enough to cover rent, food and utilities. With Uni and boxing, I don't have time to go job hunting and I want to get back into my music again.

It pains me that my guitar is sitting in my room gathering dust when I ache to play the strings again.

Anni had always loved when I played for her, so I knew that was part of the reason I'd not picked it up in months.

Even with everything else going on, sleeping with
Bella and my feelings for Kaden, I love Anni still and I
don't know when or if I'm ever going to move on.

Stepping back from the noticeboard I walk away
apprehensively, looking around to see if anyone is
going to take one.
From the other side of the room, as I try to not look
stupid backing down the hallway, the pretty brunette
steps up shyly to the board.
She looks around as though she's making sure no one
sees her reach up to the ad.

A sweet smile crosses her lips as she rips one off, and
it makes my heart skip as she clutches it in her hand
like it's something precious.
Smiling she walks away and again my heart skips
forward a bit, giving me a kinda giddy feeling that she
now has my number, even though we've never
spoken a word to each other.

~~

After uni, I'm floating on a cloud at boxing. It's an
extra practice and only a few of the guys are around.
I've barely spoken to Kaden since he left my house
after the threesome so I'm glad to find him alone in

the locker room after practice as I feel like we need to chat, man to man.

Grabbing my bag out to pack up my gloves I say to him, "I put up the roommate ad on the Uni noticeboard."

He looks straight at me, a smirk on his face when he replies, "Yeah any bites? You know my offer still stands."

"Yeah I know Kad...but after our hot but awkward threesome I don't think you moving in is a good idea."

"Yeah I know," he replies licking his lips suggestively, "any other bites?"

"Yeah, um the girl from the club I was telling you about."

"Oh shit really?" He replies, sounding a little hurt at my excitement of her having my number.

"Yeah, she looked pretty happy about taking it."

Kaden laughs, "Could you handle living with two girls again?"

I laugh then, "Maybe...I could have a different kinda threesome."

"You're so fucking dirty Aust," he teases with the same suggestive smirk on his face.

"Yeah well so are you," I tease back, "thinking about Bella's younger sister right after you fucked Bella."

"I know...I shouldn't have said anything but I've..." He cuts his own words off biting down on his lip as though dirty as fuck thoughts are running through his mind.

"What?" I laugh, not sure if I really want to know his dirty thoughts.

He runs a hand through his blonde hair. "I've not been able to get the look on her face of catching us pashing out of my mind," he confesses.

"Really?" I ask confused at what he's actually implying about Elyse.

"Yeah really...the innocence and want in her eyes; fuck it turned me on."

Playfully I punch him in the chest, looking down to his crotch and smiling at him, "You're always turned on Kad."

"Mmm, yeah around you and after our threesome as much as I liked fucking Bella I loved the moments with you more."

"Kad don't," I snap, swallowing hard before I continue, "you know I like you, but being with you confuses me."

He grabs my cock in his grip, stepping closer to me, making my breath hitch in my chest when he speaks, "Face it Aust, your bi."

"So what if I am?" I question him, feeling as though he's expecting me to confess my feelings for him.

"Enjoy it, Aust," he suggests as he licks his lips, "let how you feel in the moment take over."
I contemplate his words for a moment before winking at him and grabbing his cock as I lean in to kiss his neck.
Kissing up his neck, reaching his ear I bite his earlobe before brushing my lips against his ear and whispering, "Fancy getting wet together?"
I look at him waiting for a response and feel his cock growing in my grip.
His words of response turn me on, "What if someone catches us, Aust?"

I have to play on what he's mentioned before, so I taunt him, "Let them, being caught is half the fun remember?"
"Fuck yeah!" He replies kissing me hard, taking my breath away and sending my cock skyward.

Hastily we undress each other, dakking each other eagerly as though we can't wait for a second longer to be naked.

Frantically with no clothes between us, we kiss, tongues fighting against each other in their own boxing match.

It's hot and exciting.

Still, with our lips locked I push my hands against his chest to push him into the open shower cubicle.

His back collides with the cold tiles and he lets out a delicious moan that makes my cock rise more, his kiss is becoming more urgent as he bites my lip.

I have a feeling that we weren't going to just kiss and touch each other this time and the fact we could get caught out at any moment is setting me on fire.

Twenty-Six | Steamy Shower Experiences

Kaden

"I just want to kiss you for a while," Austin says softly into my ear reaching behind me and turning the water on.

For a moment it's cold before the hot water kicks in and the warm spray cascades over our bodies.

Wrapping my arms around his back, pulling him closer I suck on his neck, licking the water droplets off.

I can feel our aching cocks brushing against each other, pulsating with need. I pull back from kissing his neck when I feel him grabbing my cock in his grip.

He starts stroking it, up and down in a steady rhythm.

"God Aust, I love your hands on me."

His eyes lock on mine, filled with lust when he asks, "Kad, can I suck you off?"

"What Aust seriously? The other night though you...you already did."

"Yeah I know but you sucked me off though before the threesome too and I...I."

"Don't Aust...don't please....just..." He cuts my words
off with a hot kiss, licking and biting my lower lip.
I can feel my cock pulsating in his strong grip and
moan as he licks down over my chin and Adam's
apple.

Looking at me as he's still stroking my cock I scream,
"Fuck Aust, that feels good."
He laughs, smirking at me as his trail of kisses heads
further down my wet body, his licking now
collecting water droplets from my chest.
His tongue teasingly runs over my nipples, in
tantalising circles that is turning me on so bad I want
to take things to the next level.
He's now at my stomach, swirling kisses across the
flesh whilst still pumping his hand up and down on
my cock.
Reaching the v of my hips he licks each side looking
up at me for a moment, winking, before his mouth
replaces his hand on my cock.
I can't help but let out a whimper of pleasure, "God
Austin, that is so fucking good. Your mouth on me,
fuck man."

He moans as he continues the same sweet torture of
swirling his tongue everywhere on my cock, into the

tip, running it along the slit and lapping the pre-cum pearling there. As much as it feels amazing, I want more.

Grabbing his fiery red hair in my fists I pull him off my cock and he looks at me with a questioning look as he stands up.

"Aust?' I ask touching his cheek.

"What Kad?"

"Can I fuck you?" I ask, grabbing his arse cheeks in my palms.

He bites his lip, his eyes showing a mix of fear and lust.

"I don't know Kad...I'm scared it will hurt like a bitch."

I smile at him, "At first it might, but I promise I'll take it slow."

Again he bites his lip, "Ok, so um..."

I kiss him to calm his nerves, running my hands over the soft taut skin of his arse before slowly inserting a finger into his hole. He flinches a little, breaking the kiss.

"Trust me, Aust," I suggest grabbing the bottle of body wash from behind me.

It's of all things Lynx Africa scented, but anything is better than nothing right now. Squeezing some into my palm I lather it up and run it all over his body with my eyes locked on his.

"Mmm, Kad," he moans at my touch.

About to kiss him again I step back out of the shower, hearing what sounds like footsteps coming into the locker room.

"Did you hear that?" I hiss.

"No," he says shaking his head.

I'm nervous, even though the thrill of getting caught is exciting, I don't actually want it to happen.

I grab a towel, wrapping it around my waist, giving him a quick kiss as I step out of the shower.

"Wash the soap off, I'm just going to check something out. I'll be right back."

He smiles, as he starts to run his hands over his body under the water, paying extra attention to stroking his cock to wash away the soap and make his cock spring to attention.

The footsteps are coming closer, about to enter the locker room and I practically freeze when coach walks in.

"Hi Kaden, just you here?" he asks, looking at me cautiously and the tent at the front of the towel.

I know I'm blushing when I reply, "Ah yeah. I was just about to take a shower."

"No worries. I'm heading out, can you lock up tonight?"

"Yeah sure coach," I reply, one hand hopelessly trying to cover the bulge in the towel and the other in my hair.

"Have a good night Kaden," he replies winking as he walks away.

Fuck that was close

Heading back to the shower I stop by my locker to grab out a condom and the silicone lube I'd had hiding in the bottom of my bag for months, wondering if I'd ever get to use it.

I can't believe I'm going to be using it for the first time with Austin, my best mate and I'm going to fuck him hard until he screams my name.

Dropping the towel outside the shower cubicle I rip open the condom and slide it onto my aching cock before stepping up behind Austin in the shower.

I press my cock against his arse, kissing his neck again.

"Was there someone here?" he asks.

"Yeah, but all good. It's just us now," I tell him before he turns his head back to kiss me.

As we kiss I continue teasing his arse with the tip of my cock, grabbing his hard as steel cock in my fist and stroking it furiously.

I've been with other guys recently, but it has never felt this good. Austin drives me wild and when he breaks the kiss, his breathless raspy words nearly send me over the edge, "I'm ready for you to fuck me Kad."

"Fuck Aust!" I bellow, bending down to grab the lube. Squeezing some out I rub a little on the condom before touching his arse, inserting my finger inside to lube him up.

"Mmm, Kad, that feels good," he moans.

"Really Aust?"

"Really, really good," he hisses biting down on his lip looking back at me as I step closer lining my cock up with his arse, the tip just on the precipice of entering him.

"Are you sure Aust?"

"Yes," he hisses pushing his arse back against me.

Grabbing his waist, I slowly slide inside him watching his eyes as they glass over with the pain and then pleasure.

"God, Aust, fuck you feel good around my cock."

Steadily I slip my cock in and out, the absolute sheer pleasure vibrating through my whole body.

"God Kad, what are you doing to me?"

"Fucking your brains out," I laugh, "tell me how it feels Aust."

He moans, "I can't...fuck it...it feels...ah...fuck...so damn good."

"Mmm, yeah," I moan short on words.

Again he turns his head back to kiss me, so hard my cock throbs inside him.

I grab his cock, stroking it as we kiss and fuck recklessly like life depends on us reaching our release.

Droplets of pre-cum bead on the end of his cock and breaking the kiss I bring my fingers to my lips, licking it from them as Austin looks at me lustfully.

"You taste good Aust," I tease, slamming my cock balls deep into him, making him moan so loud it reverberates off the walls.

He grabs his cock, fisting it as I pump into his arse.

Reaching around his body, pulling him so close I fondle his balls in my hands.

"Kaden!" he screams out my name, "Kaden! I'm gonna cum, fuck I'm gonna cum!"

His white-hot release shoots out of his cock all over the shower wall, as I slam into him one last time, my own release spurting out hard, "Fuck Austin! I love you!"

Pulling out of his spent body I roll off the condom, dropping it to the shower floor as I kiss him again.

He breaks the kiss, looking at me so lustfully I want to take him again.

"Kad, that was amazing. I can't even tell you how much."

"I told you," I laugh as I turn off the taps and grab my towel from the floor.

Austin grabs one from the rack on the wall, wrapping it around his waist as he follows me out of the shower.

Slipping the towel from my waist I towel dry my hair, watching Austin as he starts to dress.

"Aust, are you sure you're ok?"

"Yeah, I'm great, why?"

"Because Aust, that was a big step. We just fucked Austin."

"I know and I..."

"What?" I ask, afraid to step closer for fear he's going to break my heart.

"Next time, I want to be the one fucking you." He doesn't meet my gaze, but I can't help but gape at his suggestion of this not being a one-time thing.

"Next time?"

"Yeah, next time. I like being with you Kaden."

"Really? Because you know I love being with you Austin. I'm in love with you so bad."

Slipping his t-shirt over his head he replies, "I can't tell you that I'll ever feel that way about you Kad, but I want to be with you."

"So mates with benefits then?" I ask teasingly, winking at him.

"Something like that," he laughs, slapping a hand on my back as he slings his bag over his shoulder to leave.

"Are you heading out?"

"Yeah, I'll catch ya tomorrow."

"No worries Aust. Have a good night."

He kisses me as he passes me, a lingering kiss that brushes against my lips and makes my heart pound. I really hope that the more we're together that his feelings will change and he'll fall for me too. I really want to hear 'I love you Kaden' fall from his lips.

Twenty-Seven | Pretty Sweet Words

Leaving boxing, after the incredible sex with Kaden in the shower my head is spinning.

I know that without a doubt I'm bi now and I really like how being with Kaden makes me feel different than when I'm with a girl.

He knows what turns me on, knows how to make a guy feel good and experimenting together with a guy as hot as Kaden is pretty ripper.

Nearly at home, I hear my phone vibrating in my bag on the seat beside me. It's just past seven thirty and I wonder who would be messaging me.

I'm not even sure if Bella is even home and I don't really want to face her.

My heart lurches as I pull the Ute up outside our apartment, hoping the text isn't going to be from Bella showing me a positive pregnancy test or telling me that we need to talk.

Dropping my bag inside the door, I unzip it to grab my phone out and a number I don't know has sent me a message.

My heart skips wondering if it's her, the pretty brunette.

Carefully I slide my finger across the screen and open it.

Unknown: Hi

Austin: Hi who is this?

Unknown: um someone from uni

Austin: oh you took my number?

Unknown: yeah is that ok?

Austin: why wouldnt it be?

Unknown: i saw you put it up on the board

Austin: cool so um...whats your name?

After asking the mysterious person their name, no other reply comes. I have a feeling it's her but I can't be sure. Walking into the kitchen I have a giddy smile on my face at the prospect.

"What are you smiling about?" Bella asks as she sips on her chocolate milk.

"I um...just got these texts from a random number. I put the ad up on the board today."

"Oh ok, cool," she replies as I hold my phone up to her, "Seems like a girl."

"Yeah, I think I know who it is."

"You gonna tell me?"

"Nope," I laugh.

"Oh so we have secrets from each other Austin?" she taunts me sipping her chocolate milk again and eye fucking me at the same time.

"What's got you so horny that you're eye-fucking me Bel?"

"Nothing," she snaps back.

"Sure Bel. I'd say you're still jealous of watching me with Kaden."

"Am not!" she says defensively.

"Right? So if I told you I was with him tonight, and I liked it, you wouldn't be at all jealous?"

"No, you can be with him if you're...you know...into fucking guys," she says innocently but with a seductive tone.

"And if I am into that? You won't love me anymore?" I ask pouting.

She jumps off the stool, nearly spilling her milk when she replies, "I don't love you Austin."

I touch her lips with my finger and her tongue darts out to lick it.

"Really Bella? I thought you were going to yell out I love you when I fucked you sideways the other day."

"I wasn't....I...they..."

"You're not making any sense Bel."

"Yeah, well, at least I'm not denying my sexuality."

I laugh, "I'm not Bel. I'm one hundred percent bisexual," I drawl out the word bisexual, winking at her.

She ponders my words for a moment, "How do you honestly know that now?"

"Kaden said some pretty sweet words to me," I wink, "before he fucked me."

She pushes her hands against my chest, "Eww Austin! I didn't need to hear that! Seriously! Watching you pashing was hot, but thinking of him fucking you is just yuk!"

She claps a hand to her mouth, putting her milk down on the bench as she rushes to the bathroom.

I hear her throw up again and wait a moment before following her.

"Bel?" I ask, leaning on the door jamb, not sure if I should set foot in the bathroom.

"Don't Austin, ok? I'm fine. I think it's just a stomach bug."

I don't want to pester her, but I know it's no stomach bug that's making her chunder.

I know that this time around a little stick is going to show two lines, not one.

I should have been more careful and not always listened to my cock.

Having sex with a guy definitely has some advantages, but I don't want to never be with a girl again and I quite frankly don't want to be with Bella again even though sex with her is always hot.

I want the pretty brunette.

If the text messages are from her I'm intrigued by her out of character shyness.

Twenty-Eight | Sexy Couch Playtime

For the past week I've been walking on eggshells
around Bella. She is deliberately shutting me out,
going to work and going straight to her room when
she's home.

I'd heard her getting up to vomit a few times when I
was heading out to Uni and boxing.

It scares me, as it's blindly obvious she's pregnant,
but she's denying it.

I have no doubts it's most likely mine, but at the
same time I can't be sure she'd not slept with
someone else. It's a sick cruel case of de' ja' vu' over
and over again.

Anni last year, and one of my random hookups from
high school.

Thankfully neither of them had actually been
pregnant, although I'd wanted Anni to be as I'd
hoped it would have meant we'd have been together
and she'd not have fallen for Jairus *'fucking'* Brooks.
Now I'd sorted out my odd sexual feelings, I could
kinda see why she fell for him at least from a physical
sense.

Facing my feelings explained a lot about how I'd reacted to Jairus in our house and I had Kaden, my best guy mate to thank for helping me come out of the closet.

I want to tell Anni, as she often teased me when I mentioned that I thought a guy was hot. I'd always laughed it off, but it kinda hurt deep down inside.

Speaking of Kaden he'd not been at practice for the last week since our shower experience and I missed him so much I'd jacked off thinking about our hot sexual chemistry.

Not having Uni today, I'm lying around on the couch like a slob and thoughts of Kaden are making the tent rise in my daks. Standing up from the couch I grab my phone to text him a selfie.

I type *'Missing you Kad'* before opening the camera and sending him a picture of myself wearing my favourite black Jockey boxers.

After grabbing a coke from the fridge I flop down on the couch again, flicking on the Switch to lose myself in some Super Mario Odyssey. I've barely gotten past the opening screens when my phone buzzes on the coffee table with a call.

Kaden's picture is flashing on the screen.

"Hey Kad, where ya at? I fucking miss you man."

"Um, yeah sorry Aust. I've um...not been up to practice this week."

"Did I do something wrong?"

"Nah mate, we're good."

"Are you sure Kad?"

"Yes Aust, I'm sure. That pic is hot man. Did you just take it?"

"Yeah, I'm on the couch home alone thinking about you."

I hear his breath hitch before he replies, "Really?"

"Really man. Are you busy?"

"Nah, are you down?"

"What's that mean?"

He laughs deeply, sending a jolt to my cock, "You know exactly what that means Aust."

"Oh right, yeah," I laugh realising that he's asking if I'm down to hookup.

"So?" Kaden asks huskily.

"I'm down, come over."

"Sweet, I'll be there in fifteen. Got my license back the other day."

"Sweet man, see ya soon."

He hangs up, and I gulp down the rest of my coke quickly, crushing the can in my fist as thoughts of Kaden fill my mind.

My cock hardens instantly, trying to break out through the buttonhole in my Jockey boxers.

Chuckling I flip it out over the elastic and wrap my fist around it, stroking gently.

It seems like only a few minutes pass when I hear knocking on the front door.

Standing up, without even putting my cock back into my underwear, I answer the door. Kaden looks at me lustfully, grabbing my cock in his grip as he walks inside.

"Hey Aust," he greets me huskily, "want some help with this?"

I laugh, "fuck yeah man."

He starts stroking my cock, teasing the tip with his thumb as he presses a carnal kiss to my lips, deepening it with his tongue boxing with mine.

Biting his lip, pulling it between my teeth he moans as we step back towards the couch. His hands leave my cock to push me down on the couch before he dives over me kissing me again so hard my cock throbs.

Breathlessly I pull back, "Kad...suck...me."

He doesn't reply instead kisses along the trail of hair under my belly button, before dakking me, sliding my boxers down my thighs. He licks his lips, moaning as he takes my cock into his mouth.

I throw my hands behind my head, watching him as he bobs up and down on my cock with his eyes locked on mine. His tongue swirls across the slit, lapping up the pre-cum that pearls there.

His moans and pace are frantic, driving me closer with every lick.

"Mmm...fuck...Kad...so....fuck...good," I growl biting down on my lip as he grabs my balls in his fist, fondling them and pushing his mouth further down until I graze the back of his throat.

Pulling all the way off, he touches my lips with a finger that I lick when he demands, "Come Aust, I want to taste you."

He slides back onto my cock, again pushing down to take me all the way between his hot lips and I can feel my cock throb, spasming as my load streams down his throat.

Taking his lips from me, he swallows hard and I watch his Adam's apple bob before I pull him down for a kiss.

I can feel his throbbing cock pressing against my stomach.

"Want me to return the favour?"

"Nah, I'm hoping we can head to your bedroom," he suggests.

"Yeah, for what?"

"The next time you promised me. I want to come whilst you fuck me Aust."

I laugh, pulling him down to lay next to me. I give him a soft kiss, "Sounds hot, but give me a minute yeah?"

He laughs so deeply, my cock starts to spring to attention again. He kisses me again, and we pash for a bit, our hands teasing each other's cocks.

When he breaks the kiss, his breathing is raspy, "I'd give you a lifetime Aust. I fucking love you so much."

"Kad, please. I love this, being with you, but I..."

"I know Aust, ok...I just want to be with you."

"That I can do," I chuckle, "how about we head to the bedroom?"

He kisses me again, hard, before he stands up grabbing my hand to lead me away.

My boxers fall down my legs and I step out of them, leaving them on the floor as we head down the hallway to my bedroom.

My cock is already hard as steel again thinking about what fucking Kaden again is going to feel like.

My mind also wonders if I could actually fall for him, when being with him feels so good and no unwanted consequences come from making each other come.

Twenty-Nine | It Can't Be

Bella

I've been avoiding Austin like he has the plague.

Essentially he has given me the plague, as I knew the second day I was sick after the threesome with him and Kaden that the possibility of being pregnant was real.

I tried to think back to when it could have happened, as I'd been taking my pill religiously but nothing was ever fail-safe.

So many emotions are running through my mind, a roller coaster I want off of.

It's stupid to turn up again to his doorstep, after the last time I'd attempted to face up to my feelings but I feel like he is the only one I can confide in.

Anni is going to hate me, as she is most likely going to have a heavily pregnant maid of honour and I'm too scared to tell Austin as well, just in case I blurt out my feelings for him too.

As usual, only a moment or so after knocking on the door Jax opens it shirtless. This time he's wearing 'The Flash' flannelette pyjama pants.

Laughing I speak quickly, "Hey Jax, you answer the door like the flash."

"Hey Bel," he says softly ushering me inside, before he asks, "you ok?"

"Um, no, not really. I need to tell you something."

"Ok, do you want a drink? A Beer maybe? I don't have much else."

Shaking my head, I swallow hard, "I um...would..but I can't for...um..."

"Sorry what Bel?" He asks walking across the room and grabbing out a beer from the fridge for himself. Flicking the top off he takes a sip, again asking, "Are you sure you don't want one?"

"I cant Jax. Have you got tea? Or Orange juice maybe?"

"Um, no...since when do you drink tea, Bel?"

"Since coffee smells so rotten, it makes me want to spew."

My words hit him, the realisation in his mind making him spit his beer out in a flustered sputter.

"What the fuck Bel! You're shitting me yeah?"

"No Jax, I'm not," I reply, fishing through my bag for the pregnancy test I'd taken before I'd come over. I follow him as he walks to the lounge room and sits on the couch.

I hold up the pregnancy test for him to see and an odd expression flashes in his brown eyes.

"Fuck Bel! How many weeks?"

"I don't know. I only just found out a couple of days ago, but a month or so I'm guessing."

"God, Bel, I don't know what to say. Is it mine? Is that why you're telling me?"

Sighing, I can't meet his eyes when I reply, "I don't know Jax, maybe."

"Maybe? So it could be someone else's?"

"Yeah Austin's," I mutter lifting my head to see his reaction.

"Well, I...um...we always used protection Bella, plus you being on the pill, yeah?"

"Yeah, but there was that one night when the condom broke remember?"

"Shit yeah, I forgot about that. Did you um...use protection with him?"

I shake my head, feeling super guilty, as even though Jaxon and I had a condom mishap, it was one time.

This baby is Austins', I know it as we've had unprotected sex more times than I care to admit to myself.

"Bella, how could you be so careless!"

Tears sting my eyes and I stammer, "I...I..I don't know, but I...I."

"What Bel? I'm here for you. Tell me," he says softly, putting his beer bottle down on the coffee table and lightly touching my arm.

"I'm in love with him."

"Aww shit Bel," he says loudly, pouting, "You need to tell him."

"I cant. He's still in love with Anni and I don't think he feels the same way about me."

"He's an idiot Bel if he doesn't feel that way about you."

"Jax don't please."

"It's true Bel. I meant it when I said I love you. I know your mouth was around my cock but I'm telling you I really do fucking love you, Bella."

"But Jax, I...I..."

"I know. I get it ok? But if you need me to help you raise this kid, whether it's mine or not, I'm all in."

"Thanks. Can I stay with you tonight?"

He laughs softly, "You can stay as long as you need gorgeous."

"Thanks, Jax. I really appreciate it."

He smiles, tucking a stray piece of hair behind my ear before leaning over to kiss my forehead.

"Bel?" He asks softly resting his forehead on mine as he shuffles closer to me on the couch.

"Yeah?" I ask, my lips so close to his I'd barely have to move an inch to kiss him.

"Can I kiss you?"

I don't reply, instead close the gap between us by kissing his lips softly.

It isn't anything like kissing Austin, not heart pounding, not butterflies in my belly, but it still makes my body react and as Jaxon kisses me back it's clear he isn't lying about his feelings for me.

I only wish I could return them and hope that maybe if this baby is his that in time I will.

Loving Austin I know in my head is a straight shot to heartbreak.

Thirty | Little Blue Bubbles

Getting home from boxing, I find Bella not home and the house feels icy. It isn't officially winter for a week or so but the chill factor has definitely settled on Melbourne.

Dropping my bag by the door I rush straight to the lounge room to start the fire.

Flicking the switch, the bright blue flame flares up instantly creating a glowing warmth.

It isn't a traditional wood fireplace, like the one in my parents place that I'd burnt my arse on as a kid, but the fake gas log fireplace still warms our little apartment well.

Flopping back on the couch, I close my eyes for a minute, thinking about the mess I've gotten myself into.

Kaden is being all lovey, dovey, wanting to pash like twenty-four seven, among other things and even though I enjoy being with him in a physical sense I still only see him as my mate, my guy best mate.

I know it's wrong to be fucking him and fucking with his emotions, but it's blocking out my emotions.

In the moments I'm with him or Bella, amidst pleasure, no thoughts of Annika fill my mind.

Stupidly I've even watched a few football games on TV just to see her on the screen, cheering Jairus on in the cheer squad.

It's torture, as his name is mentioned what seems like literally every five minutes.

It makes me want to reach into the screen to punch him. Even putting the tv on mute doesn't help shield me from the torture as he flashes up on the screen so much it's like he is the only player on the team.

About to inflict the torture on myself again I clutch the tv remote in my hand, pressing the on button.

I'm faced with a blank screen, so grab my switch controller instead to lose myself in some Super Mario Odyssey.

A couple of minutes later, my phone buzzes in my back pocket.

Kaden's picture is flashing on the screen. Him calling only means one thing and another hookup is the last thing I need.

I want to block out all thoughts of the hot as fuck sex we'd had last time he came over.

I can't see my Dad being happy if I brought a boyfriend home to meet the family, rather than a girlfriend.

Going back to my game, I leave my phone resting on the coffee table.

Kaden doesn't call again, but my phone is taunting me, not going to the lock screen.

Picking it up again I decide to text the random number from the other day, wanting to find out if it really is the pretty brunette.

Austin: are you there?

Unknown: yes i'm here...sorry about the other day

Austin: it's ok

Unknown: i just really wanted to talk to you

Austin: why didn't you?

Unknown: i...um

Austin: what?

Unknown: im too shy

Austin: are you brunette by any chance?

Unknown: how did you know that?

Austin: i saw you taking my number and...

Unknown: omg

Austin: you're really pretty

Unknown: don't say that...

Austin: why?

Unknown: because...

Austin: thats not a reason

Unknown: do you really want to know my name?

Austin: i'll tell you mine if you tell me yours?

Unknown: It's Dana...

Austin: Nice to meet you Dana...I'm Austin lol

Her replies stop then, the little typing bubbles
stopping and starting on the screen.

In my mind now, I'm starting to piece together when
I'd seen her and it's beginning to make sense.

She'd been at our party last year, with Jairus' best
mate, and I'd seen her sometimes cheering alongside
Anni.

Up until our first encounter at Uni though I'd not
seen her around any other time.

It's clear she is with Jairus' best mate and I don't like
how much knowing that hurts my feelings.

I don't even know her, but I desperately want to.

~~

A week or so passes and i've not heard a word from
Dana nor seen Bella for more than a minute, as she
flitted in and out, grabbing some clothes before she
was out the door without even a hello.

I know something is definitely up with her, and it's
pissing me off that she's deliberately shutting me out.

She is thankfully still paying her rent, but the house is super lonely without her around and it isn't the sex I'm missing, but just having someone else in the house, someone else to talk to.

As though she is feeling exactly the same, my phone buzzes with a text.
Leaning back on the kitchen bench, I smile seeing her name on my screen.

Dana: Hi Austin
Austin: Hey pretty brunette
Dana: don't tease me
Austin: im not Dana
Dana: ...
Austin: dots huh? Lol!
Dana: i don't know what to say
Austin: tell me about yourself
Dana: what do you want to know?

The typing dots appear again, going on and off the screen. It's sweet torture.
I send another text back and her reply makes me laugh out loud.

Austin: anything

Dana: um…I like dogs

Austin: lol you're cute Dana, are you normally this shy?

Dana: no…only with you

Austin: me? why me?

Dana: i like you

Austin:send me a pic :)

Dana: …..

The second I send the words *'send me a pic'* and her response of dots comes through I want to press delete.

She is going to think I'm a complete douche, only after sex and that is honestly the last thing I want from her.

Thirty-One | Asking Too Much

Dana

Getting Austin's text about sending him a picture of myself makes my heart flutter.

It's stupid, but I feel like I'm falling for him.

His messages are flirty and he makes me feel like I could let my guard down.

Guys always get the wrong impression of me, as I basically just throw myself at anyone willing after breaking up with my boyfriend Ben.

His cheating on me, made me guard my heart and it's easier to just be with a guy than to worry about feelings.

But I like Austin, which makes me feel shy around him because I want more than a casual hookup from him.

His request has thrown me off, as it seems as though he is just like any other guy.

My reply is supposed to throw him off completely, but it doesn't.

Dana: I cant im in pjs
Austin: sounds hot...please...

Reluctantly, I send him a picture, in my pink and black singlet pyjama top. It lifts my cleavage up into perfect mounds.

Dana: is that good?
Austin: good? fuck Dana...you're gorgeous
Dana: really?
Austin: how do you not know? i saw you at Rivera a few weeks ago. you didn't seem shy pashing a guy on the dance floor
Dana: um yeah...i um
Austin: what?
Dana: i can't tell you...you won't like me if I do

His words shock me a little, as he seems to be showing me that maybe he does like me. I'd not seen him on the night he was referring to, but I know when it was and it was the last time I'd slept over at Travis' house.

He'd taken me out to escape my roommates who'd decided to have a party involving all sorts of drugs and I didn't want any part of it.

Austin's reply is sweet and makes my heart flutter again. I'm in big trouble but wonder as I continue texting him whether I'm asking too much from him. Part of me wants to be blunt with him and tell him to ask me out, but it feels too forward so I explain more about Travis instead.

Austin: i doubt that Dana

Dana: that was Travis...we just hook up sometimes

Austin: really? so he's not your boyfriend?

Dana: no do you have a girlfriend?

Austin: um...no...not exactly

Dana: what's that mean?

Austin: you won't like me if I tell you...so let's leave it there

Dana: ok :)

He doesn't reply to my emoji, so I leave my phone on the kitchen bench to charge whilst I head to the bathroom to get ready for bed.

It's only just past seven pm, but I'm planning an early night in bed with a book.

My roommates have all gone somewhere else for the night, or wouldn't be back until some ungodly hour. I also want to get some sleep before then, as they usually bring a bed buddy home and go at it until morning, their screams and moans torture to my ears even if I bury my head under my pillow. It's a curse of living in an old rundown house on campus with paper thin walls.

I hear my phone ping with another text, just as I'm finishing up from brushing my teeth. Picking it up from the kitchen bench, there is another text from Austin.

Austin: we good?
Dana: yeah
Austin: are you sure?
Dana: yep im not going to ask about your relationship status no more
Austin: shit Dana...I didn't mean to upset you
Dana: you didn't...im fine
Austin: i hope so...i'll text you 2moro. gotta go...have a good night gorgeous!
Dana: Goodnight Austin! :)

Again he hasn't said anything like asking me out.

I take my phone to my bedroom, sliding into bed and pulling the covers up to my neck.

It's freezing, so snuggling deeper under the covers I close my eyes, trying not to think about the fact that I'm falling for Austin and I barely even know the guy.

I desperately want to know him, but that is probably asking too much.

Thirty-Two | Cheshire Cat Smiles

Kaden

Something is different with Austin since our last hook up. I'm angry at myself for thinking with my cock, when my heart is involved, but just having Austin in my life even if he doesn't or won't ever feel the same way is better than not having him in my life at all.

After practice we again find ourselves alone in the locker room.

My mind is wondering to dirty thoughts again and I can't help but smile.

"What are you smiling about Kad?" Austin asks in a cheeky tone.

"Just thinking about our last time alone here. You?"

"Dana's been messaging me," he replies, pulling his phone out of his gym bag.

The way he says her name, the wide smile that graces his face makes me feel a little upset.

He is staring at the phone screen when I ask, "Are you falling for her man? I've not seen a Cheshire cat smile on your face in ages."

He laughs, looking up at me, his eyes smiling, "No Kad I don't even know her...we've only texted each other."

"So..."

"There's no so about it," he interjects.

"You want to know her...you're licking ya fucking lips looking at something on ya phone."

"Am not," he defends, biting down on his lip this time.

Elbowing him in the side I snatch his phone from his fingers. The words and image on the open screen is hot and makes me a little excited, but upset at the same time.

On the screen are teasing words from Austin, asking her to send another pic and below his words she'd sent a picture of herself posing in her black underwear seductively with one hand behind her head. She is gorgeous; perfect rounded breasts, flat as stomach and wide hips.

Handing his phone back, after a little tussle of keepers off, I say, "Fuck Aust...she's a knockout. I thought you said she was shy."

"Well, I don't know...she was at first when we started texting but she's never seemed shy otherwise."

I laugh at not only his words, but the blush that rises up his cheeks, "Hmm," I mutter, "shy girls, don't send hot guys pics in their underwear Aust."

He laughs, "Yeah...true."

It hurts like knives to the heart to even think of asking the next question, but I open my mouth anyway, "Aust do you like her?"

"Yeah I think she's hot as fuck Kad," he replies, not able to wipe the grin from his face.

"Then ask her out," I suggest, breaking my own heart more.

"You think I should? Would you be upset?"

"Of course I would be, but it's just a date, Aust. She might even turn you down."

"Haha, funny."

"Have you sent her any pics?" I ask, wondering if she's seen how insanely hot he is underneath his clothes.

"No, she knows what I look like," he laughs.

I laugh in response, teasing him with my words, "Yeah but not what you look like underneath your clothes, Aust."

He smiles wide, winking at me, "For now only you get that privilege Kad."

I can't help myself, when he looks at me, I kiss him, hard, pushing him back against the lockers as I run my his hands up under his t-shirt.

Deepening the kiss he moans against my lips, sending my cock high, brushing against his thigh.

Breaking apart for a moment I joke when a wide smile spreads across his lips, "There's that Cheshire cat smile again. I love you Austin."

He punches me playfully in the stomach, "Stop it, Kaden! I like, like you."

Hearing him say those words isn't the exact ones I want to hear, but they still excite me a lot.

There is promise in them and again I kiss him, about to take the kiss further again when we hear footsteps entering the locker room.

I hate having to be always on my guard around our mates and coach, hiding that there is something going on between us, but I'm not ready for anyone to know I'm in love with my best guy mate.

It hurts even more that he doesn't want to take our relationship out of the shadows into the real world, but as another mate enters the room and Austin grabs his stuff out of his locker to head out, the wide Cheshire cat smile on his face directed at me gives me hope as he walks out.

Thirty-Three | Baby Not Shy

Dana

I feel a little nervous knocking on Travis's door. It's been weeks since I've seen him, as the Tigers had a couple of away games and I'd not been down to the rooms after the games either.

I was avoiding him, but he text me out of the blue telling me he missed me, which for Travis meant he wanted to hookup.

Commitment and relationships weren't in his vocabulary. It's just sex with him, and as much as I enjoy it I want more.

Startling me, he opens the door wearing only dark denim jeans hanging low on his hips.

Damn him to hell for looking so fucking gorgeous

They expose his tattoos that are scattered over his torso. I lick my lips, gulping as he ushers me inside. "Damn baby, why wear something so hot if I'm just taking it off you?" he practically groans, his eyes looking me up and down, taking in my short blue halter neck dress, all the way down to my thongs.

"Because you're not taking it off me Trav," I inform him with a teasing tone.

"What do you mean, baby?" he asks pouting at me like a damn child who's just been told they can't have chocolate.

"I want you to take me out on a date, a proper date," I declare eagerly.

"You know I don't do the whole date thing, Dan," he tells me defiantly, his hands on his hips.

"Yeah, well I want to Trav....I miss stuff like that."

He stares at me for a moment, contemplating what I'm asking, before he sighs, running a hand through his dark ash blonde locks, "Fine, come in...give me a minute."

He scoots down the hallway, coming back practically a second later slipping his arms thru his t-shirt sleeves.

At the door he pulls some sneakers onto his feet and smiles at me.

"Ready, baby?"

"Yeah," I reply meekly.

He grabs his wallet and keys and snakes an arm around my side as he leads me out of his apartment to his car parked on the street.

~~

Half an hour later, we pull up in Travis's Jaguar outside Luna Park.
He looks around, winking at me when he asks teasingly, "So does car sex count as a date, baby?"

I shake my head at him, getting out of the car. He gets out, following me around to the other side.

"Are you up for the ghost train?" I ask him when he takes my hand.
"Are you baby? You can hang on to me anytime."
"Not funny Travis, I'm no chicken."
"Never said you were baby, but what if I am?"
I laugh at his tease. When we get to the gates, he drops my hand, stepping up to the ticket booth to pay.
From my handbag I try to hand him a fifty dollar note, but he brushes my hand away tapping his credit card on the machine to pay.

He takes my hand again, waving the unlimited ride tickets in his other hand.

I snatch mine from his grip, as we walk through the open mouth into the park.

"You didn't have to buy my ticket Travis."

"Yeah I did, Dan. I might be a dick most of the time, but I know what being chivalrous is."

I smile at him, before kissing his cheek. I like this side of him too much and as we head towards the ghost train I try to push the giddy feeling in my stomach aside.

Feeling that way about Travis is sure to be total heart anarchy.

After nearly three hours of rides and silliness like crazy teenagers we're heading back to Travis's apartment.

My stomach is still giddy, not from the rides but from how odd Travis was acting.

Normally he'd never kiss me in public, or show any kind of affection towards me in public but he'd pulled me close, hugging me multiple times, held my hand the entire time and given me sneaky knicker melting kisses on the ghost train and rollercoaster.

I should have known such affection from him though would be short lived, and a way to get into my knickers for the night.

Stupid me though, I never can resist him.

Pulling up outside his apartment, he cuts the engine, reaching over to touch my thigh.

"Baby, come in please?" he begs, his eyes locked on mine and full of lust.

"Trav please, I don't think we should."

"Oh come on Dan, you've teased me all fucking arvo," he bellows, his hand edging higher, right at the edge of my lacy knickers that are soaked with desire.

"Trav, I...I," I stammer, feeling his finger tease me through the lace.

"Come on Dan, baby, you're wet as fuck for me."

I groan, wanting to fight the temptation, but it's futile when his finger slips beneath the lace to flick my clit as he smashes a kiss to my lips.

He starts to pump his finger in and out of my dripping folds, his kiss hard and possessive, his tongue in my mouth dancing with mine in a rhythm like his finger inside me.

I feel like I'm about to come, all over the slick black leather seats of his Jag.

Panting I break the kiss, "Trav, fuck….um…"

"What baby? You can't tell me you're not loving that."

He pulls his finger out, raising it to his lips and closing his eyes as he licks it, moaning like tasting me on his finger is the most delicious taste known to man.

When he opens them a moment later, I speak again, "I um…did love it but i'm about to come all over your seats."

"Well, we can't have that. Get inside now, so I can fuck you until you purr baby," he taunts, laughing.

Before I can even think he's out of the car, and at my door, opening it with a hand outstretched to me.

Taking it I stand up and he pulls me up out of the car, into his arms.

I'm leaning against the car when he smashes a kiss against my lips, and he moans as he reaches up under the hem of my dress.

Cupping my arse cheeks in his palms, I whimper in pleasure, the kiss dirty and arousing, almost indecent considering we're still on the street outside his apartment.

Still kissing me, I feel his fingers slip beneath the elastic. He starts to edge them over my arse and I pull back from his kiss, cursing, "Fuck Trav, what are you doing?"

"Taking off your soaked knickers baby," he informs me with a snigger.

"I can see that Travis, but have you lost your mind? We're still outside!"

"I realise that Dana, and i'm going to take them off you and you can leave them in my car to remind me of you practically coming all over my seat."

I scoff, looking at him with an accusing look.

"You disgust me sometimes Travis."

"You love my dirtiness, baby. Now are you gonna take them off? Or do I have to?"

Again I scoff, stepping aside, hoisting my skirt up a little and slipping the lacy knickers down my legs. When they reach my feet, I kick them and my thongs off. Bending down to pick them up I hold them up to Travis on one finger, and he smirks when he grabs them from me, sniffing them and moaning.

"Fuck Dan baby, you soaked these knickers real good."

I feel myself blushing, his eyes on mine are full of lust, making me feel brazen when I kiss him hard.

Responding to the kiss, he throws my knickers into the open car and pulls me aside so he can shut the door.

He breaks the kiss, not saying another word, instead just drags me inside.

We're barely inside the door when Travis kisses me, furiously, backing us towards the futon couch in the middle of his small apartment.

Clothes and empty bowls are discarded around the room, making me feel a little queasy.

He pushes me down on the couch and it screeches along the floorboards a little when it moves back against the wall.

"You could clean up Travis."

"I wasn't exactly expecting company tonight, baby."

"Hmm, whatever," I mumble, when he bends down in front of me, diving under the hem of my dress.

I'm about to protest when I feel his tongue glide over my clit, and instead of protesting my body takes over and I whimper at the pleasure.

Travis is definitely skilled at using his tongue, rolling it over my clit and into my folds, lapping up my arousal.

His hands grip my hips, as he continues to lick and he pushes my dress up.

Stopping a moment, he looks up at me, smirking like a damn devil.

"Dan, baby, can you take this tight little dress off? I want to fuck you naked."

I huff, sitting up a bit on the couch so he can gather the fabric up towards my chest.

When he reaches my breasts, I pull the halter neck over my head and keep my arms up so Travis can pull the dress off me completely.

He inspects my naked body with a sinful smirk, full of lust.

"Damn Dan...baby...your body is hot as fuck...you fucking sexy minx not wearing a bra."

I mutter an 'mmm' in response, staring at him and wondering why I'm the only one without clothes on.

"Trav, you're still dressed."

He stands up, his bulging crotch at my eye level.

"Then undress me, baby," he taunts, pushing his crotch closer to me.

Standing up, I stumble a little falling into his arms. He wraps his arms around me, smashing a kiss to my lips and smiling against my mouth.

My body is reacting, my core tightening and pulling back from the kiss I giggle.

Bunching up his t-shirt I pull it over his head, throwing it on the floor.

I gaze over his chest, his rock hard ironing board abs, noticing a new tattoo I'd not seen before.

Brushing it with my fingers I ask softly, "Is this new?

"Yeah, and still a little tender baby," he hisses through gritted teeth.

"Sorry," I apologise reaching down between us to undo the belt of his jeans.

I fumble with the buttons and zip, my fingers a little shaky.

I know I shouldn't be fucking Travis again, not now when I've started flirting with Austin.

I'm feeling confused, I've got a mega crush on the gorgeous red head, but Travis can make me want to come just by looking at me.

Now Travis is standing in front of me only in tight red boxers that are bulging with his sizeable hard cock.

My mind wanders to thinking about what Austin's cock might be like, but my thoughts are broken when Travis grabs my hand, shoving it down the front of his boxers.

"Touch me baby, make my cock hard so I can fuck you into next week."

Not responding, I squeeze his cock in my hand, running my hand up and down his length, feeling him grow.

His eyes darken with lust and groaning he pulls his boxers down his legs.

"Mmm, Dan, baby, just like that," he grunts, still glaring at me with lust flashing in his eyes.

"Mmm, you like that huh?" I taunt him, smirking.

Again he grunts, before kissing me pushing me back down on the couch.

I can barely think, as he forces his cock inside me, moaning as he fills me.

Running his hands down my sides, he starts thrusting in and out, deep, hard and wild.

"Fuck, Dan, baby! You grip my cock like a fucking animal."

He crushes his lips to mine, in a kiss that is dirty and fierce, just like his cock driving into me. I can't help but let out moans of pleasure when he hits my g-spot repeatedly.

Closing my eyes I focus on the pleasure flowing through my body. I can hear his moans filling my ears, him murmuring my name.

His thrusts slow, and he purrs, "Dan, baby, come with me."

Like his words are a switch, I start to tremble feeling my climax building.

His release is sudden, filling me with warmth and I scream out, "Austin, oh fuck!", as my own release takes over.

He jumps off the couch in shock, screeching at me, "What the fuck Dana? Who the fuck is Austin?"

I shrink back on the couch, slapping a hand against my mouth as I look up at Travis who is glaring at me with anger in his eyes.

"Well? Who the fuck is he?" he bellows at me, looking like he wants to punch someone.

I bite down on my lip a moment, my heart hammering in my chest.

"He's...um...he's...a...friend."

Travis slams a fist against the couch, "A friend! A fucking friend! Really Dana? You've got to be fucking shitting me!"

Again I stammer, "I'm...I'm...not... Travis. Austin is just a friend."

I say the words but I know they are lies, I may not have officially met Austin, but I think of him as more than a friend and the fact I'd just called out his name during sex with someone else is alarming.

Travis is still glaring at me, seething with anger.
I stand up, picking up my dress from the floor. I have no words to say to him, feeling scared that he's about to hit me.

As I slip my dress back over my head he screams at me, "Get the fuck out Dana, you're a fucking skank."

I sniff back tears, rushing out of his apartment.
As I shut the door behind me I look at him sitting back down on the couch with his head in hands.
My heart hurts, but I don't know why.
The name he called me hurts, but in some ways I knew he is right about me.

As I run to the tram, I vow to myself to take things slowly with Austin and to forget about Travis. Sex isn't going to heal my heart from Ben shattering it into pieces.

Thirty-Four | Ask Her Out

Kaden's words have tumbled in my head all week. He's been pushing me to ask Dana out but at the same time it's clear he isn't going to be happy if I do ask her out. I've barely spoken to her since she sent me the last picture of herself in the sexy black underwear and I'm kicking myself for how bad that is.

She's insecure enough without my stupidity making it worse.

The more I think about it though, the more I do want to go on a date with her.

It's been a long time since I've gone on a date with anyone; being honest the last girl I went on a date with was Anni and that was back in high school. Grabbing a beer out of the fridge, I flick the top off gulping half of it down as I stare at my phone screen wondering how I should even ask her out.

We've only been texting each other, so that seems like the best option. The thought of calling her surfaces in my mind, but I know if I call I'll chicken out, hearing her voice for the first time, so instead gulping down the last of the beer I send her a text.

Austin: Dana, go on a date with me?
Dana: Really? You want to go out with me?
Austin:yeah gorgeous I do
Dana:ok Friday night?
Austin: sounds good...you do know what I look like yeah? Lol
Dana: send a pic to remind me

I send her a picture I'd taken recently wearing jeans and a white t-shirt. My arms were folded across my chest, my grin wide.

Dana:I meant a sexy one
Austin:Sorry gorgeous...after our date ;)
Dana:fine :p text me details
Austin:will do gorgeous...dream of me naked tonight :p
Dana: in your dreams Austin :p
Austin: you know it gorgeous x

Getting her responses makes me smile, especially the one about sending her a sexy picture. I'm not shy at all, but with Dana, I feel like I need to close part of myself away. It's silly, but I want her to like me for me, not for my body.

It isn't like that has happened recently, with Anni, Bella or Kaden, but it's pretty much a given with anyone else before them.

I'm a little excited at the prospect of going on a date with Dana, my mind ticking over with where to take her as I head down the hallway to my bedroom.

With no new roommate I'm struggling to keep on top of the rent, but moving out and having Kaden move in were my only other options and neither of those are particularly appealing.

I now have the typical uni student diet of cereal, two-minute noodles, coffee and Macca's. It isn't exactly good for keeping in shape, but it's keeping me alive. In my bedroom, I've shuffled the furniture around, pushing the two single beds together to make one larger one. I brought a memory foam mattress topper and some fancy cloud underlay so I can't feel the join in the middle and it's actually rather comfortable. I also bought new sheets, and a new doona with a cover that screamed little boy, as it has Spiderman on it.

I'm a kid at heart after all and stripping down to my Flash boxers I climb into bed with the perfect date in my mind.

Closing my eyes, clutching my Spiderman doona I wonder if the night out with Dana will end with a kiss, or maybe even seeing her naked, out of the sexy black lingerie.

My cock hardens at the thought and I grab it rubbing it as I fall asleep dreaming of a perfect night out ending with a perfect night in.

Caz May

Thirty-Five | Charming Date Antics

As Friday night approaches I'm feeling a little giddy, partly as I'm going to officially meet Dana and partly because I've not been to an arcade since I was like thirteen.

I've always loved video game arcades, losing hours in the local one playing pinball and trying to beat my high score on the dance battle game.

Getting ready, I laugh thinking about my geeky younger self, the nerdy gangly redhead who hid in the library and the arcade until I hit puberty and started noticing girls.

Anni never believed that I was a virgin when we met, but she was the first girl I went all the way with and my naive seventeen-year-old self honestly thought she'd be the only girl I slept with.

But fast forward five years and I've had more girls in my bed that I care to admit and then Kaden as well.

I've not been on a date for so long, since Anni, and raking a comb through my hair after I've dressed in a light blue shirt and black jeans I try to psyche myself up.

I spray my favourite cologne on, Tommy by Tommy Hilfiger and contemplate for a minute if I should've shaved.

I have the start of a five o clock shadow on my jawline. Touching it between my thumb and forefinger, I hear Anni's voice in my head, *'You look sexy with stubble on your chin Aust'.*

It makes me smile, I walk out of the bathroom grabbing my black leather jacket and ute keys on the way out the door. Dana has texted me her address, telling me her house is basically in the Swinburne university carpark. She told me she'll be waiting for me outside at precisely seven o'clock.

It's currently six twenty and thankfully it's only a fifteen-minute drive to Uni from my house.

Weaving through the traffic on Burwood Road, I crank the radio up when 'Paradise' starts playing.

To calm my nerves I start belting it out, tapping my fingers to the beat on the steering wheel.

Reaching the Uni campus, I follow the signs to the carpark like Dana has told me. The clock on the dash reads six fifty.

Pulling up in front of the little rundown cottage I can't see her.

Cutting the engine I sigh, leaning back in the seat to wait.

I'm about to toot the horn to let her know I've arrived when she steps out of the front door wearing a stunning outfit.

Knee-high black boots, fishnet tights with a bright blue mini skirt and a black jumper that has the slogan '*I wish I was Barbie, that bitch gets everything*' on the front.

I laugh smiling at her as she crosses the carpark to the ute. Her legs look even longer and my wicked mind imagines them wrapped around me as she slides into the passenger side.

My mouth feels dry, my tongue tied. Starting the engine I smile wider as I greet her, "Hey Dana. You...um...look gorgeous."

She bites down on her lip, before muttering, "Hi Austin, you um...look...um...really hot."

"Thanks, so are you ready for some fun?"

She blushes, her cheeks turning a deep shade of crimson that follows down her neck. I wonder if her skin blushes anywhere else, my eyes trying to focus on watching for oncoming traffic instead of undressing her in my mind.

"Um depends on what sort of fun you had in mind."

I laugh, teasing her with my words, "Some good old fashioned, clean fun."

Pulling back out onto Burwood Road, I wink at her when she lets out a simple 'oh' in response.

"Don't worry Dana. We'll be keeping our clothes on. You trust me?"

"Yeah, I do," she says giggling slightly and fidgeting with the strap on her handbag.

It's sweet she's so nervous. I want to do something to calm her down, but don't think that touching her practically bare thigh through the fishnet tights is a good idea.

I'm so forward with girls usually, but I know that the fact she is so shy around me means she likes me and I don't want to stuff anything up between us by moving to fast this time. I get the sense she's been hurt too.

It's a short drive to 'The Jam factory' and driving into the undercover carpark she looks across at me, asking, "Are we going to a movie?"

I slide the Ute into a car space, cutting the engine, "No we're not going to a movie Dana."

"Oh ok, good. That's so cliched."

Laughing I quickly jump out of the Ute, rushing
around to her side to open her door.

Holding out my hand, she smiles when she takes it in
hers.

A delightful tingle runs up my arm and she flinches,
telling me she feels it too.

I don't let go, instead lace our fingers together to
lead her inside, locking the Ute with the key fob in
my other hand.

Walking through the double sliding doors I ask her,
"So do you know what we're doing yet?"

"Intencity? Laser tag?"

Squeezing her hand I reply, "You guessed it gorgeous.
Are you ready to take on the dance battle master?"

She giggles, letting her guard down as she drops her
hand from mine, running backwards into Intencity.

Her brown hair is down around her shoulders
swaying from side to side in her eager state, and she
looks absolutely stunning.

"Oh you bet I am! I'm the master of dance battle,
thank you!"

At the coin machine, I insert a twenty dollar note in
exchange for tokens, taking Dana's hand again.

She stops in front of the dance battle game and I
insert the required tokens to fire up the game.

She flicks through the songs choosing one with a simple beat but fast tempo.

The music starts and she effortlessly dances the steps, whilst I stand there watching her instead of moving.

When the screen suggests us to swap sides she slides across to mine as I slide to hers, our bodies brushing against each other. The same tingle from earlier rushes through me, and her smile tells me she feels it too. Back on her side, she laughs, "You're so going to lose, Austin!"

Laughing I dance faster, trying to concentrate on the steps and not sneak glances at her dancing beside me.

When the game ends, she shrieks with joy, "Ha, told you!"

Stepping off the game, I bow to her, "I bow to thee dance master."

She laughs, holding up her hand that I high-five, before she curtsies.

"Thank you, thank you."

I'm loving how she is letting her guard down, not the shy girl who'd first texted me a few months earlier.

I'm still getting the sense that she's been hurt, so
even though the want to kiss her is desperate I'm
holding back.

Taking her hand I lead her over to the Racing
simulator.

We both slide into a seat, and she starts to turn the
wheel and shift the gears.

"You know the game hasn't started yet Dan, yeah?"

I clap a hand to my mouth, realising I've just called
her a nickname. It seems so intimate and I wish for a
moment that the racing chair would swallow me.

"I'm just practising Aust, so you don't whip me."

She laces her words with lust, my nickname and whip
sounding so illicit I feel my jeans tighten a little.

We complete two races, which I win both of.

We play a few other silly games, basketball toss,
some crazy crocodile hitting one and some others.

Somehow we've managed to collect a couple of
hundred tickets, despite being hopeless at most of
the games.

Dana is now standing at the counter, contemplating
which stuffed toy to claim when I step up behind her,
wrapping my arms around her waist.

She shifts a little in my arms, looking back at me when I whisper, "You up for a game of Laser tag, Dan?"

She pulls away from my arms, and I feel empty, wanting to pull her back to kiss her. But I wait for her reply, not wanting to push too far, too quick.

"Oh yeah, I'm up for that," she replies.

"Prepare to go down, gorgeous."

"I don't think so stud," she replies as we pay and get suited up.

My heart skips at her calling me Stud. It isn't something I've been called before, but I kind of like it.

We enter the dark laser tag room a couple of minutes later and Dana runs off in the opposite direction to me, giggling.

It's a delicious sound and I start to walk around the room, my laser gun aimed high listening for footsteps.

We've barely been in there for ten minutes when I feel the laser hit my chest and I fall down against a stack of crates.

I hear her voice in the darkness, "Haha….I…got…"

Her words are cut short when she trips over my outstretched leg, falling on top of me.

"You got me Dan," I laugh, trying to focus on looking at her in the darkness.

My heart is hammering in my chest, and I could swear hers is too. She makes no move to stand up, so I reach up to cup her cheek in my palm.

"Dan, are you ok?"

"Yep," she snaps shifting uncomfortably and standing up so quick I feel like she's shot me with a real gun, not a laser gun.

She holds out her hand to help me up, and I ask,

"Ready to go collect your victory prize?"

"Yeah," she replies, leading me away.

It's sweet that she doesn't let go of my hand.

Even once out of the dark laser tag room, and when she's telling the desk attendant that she wants the giant purple elephant toy, she is still clutching my hand with our fingers laced together.

It's a simple touch, but it feels so intimate.

Driving back to hers, there is a comfortable silence between us.

We keep glancing over at each other, me winking at her and she giggles. It's like we are silly teenagers again, and I love it.

Pulling into the uni carpark, I reach over to touch the skin of her thigh, below the hem of her mini skirt.

Her legs part a little and I edge my hand a little lower between them.

Stopping out the front of her house, I cut the engine and look across at her without moving my hand.

"Dan, I had a really great night."

"Me too Aust. I haven't had that much fun on a date in awhile."

"I'm glad," I reply smiling at her.

I lean across the console, locking my eyes on her hers, stealing a glance at her lips that curve up in a sweet smile.

She shakes her head at me, making my heart sink before she presses a soft kiss to my cheek.

"Thanks Austin, Goodnight."

"Goodnight gorgeous, do you want me to walk you in?"

"Nah, I'll be fine. Goodnight, stud," she says softly, opening her door and grabbing her stuffed elephant from beside her feet.

Shutting the door she walks quickly to her house, stopping on the porch to wave at me as I drive away.

I'm feeling a mix of emotions. It had been more fun than I'd had in ages, without alcohol and yet she shut me down for a goodnight kiss.

I wonder if I'm reading too much into the tension between us.

I want her so damn much it hurts and it's scary.

I barely know her, but after one sweet date I want her even more than before and I'm going to turn on the charm to make her mine.

Thirty-Six | Heart Beats Flicker

Jaxon

Taking Bella's hand in mine, I squeeze it reassuringly as we walk into the hospital.

"Bel, you ok babe?"

"Yeah, this just makes it real."

I stop a moment in the waiting room. Bella turns to look at me worriedly.

"Bel, you know you've still got time if you..." She glares at me as though I've struck a nerve, cutting me off with her reply, "Don't even say that Jax. I'm keeping this baby, with or without you by my side."

I don't mean to but let out a laugh, "Are you kidding me, Bella? I'm so excited to be having a baby with you."

"Really? But we....we..." she starts cutting her words off when she steps up to the desk to speak to the receptionist.

She instructs us to sit down in the chairs to the side of the desk.

Following Bella I sit down beside her, rubbing my hand up and down her thigh.

"Bel," I start waiting for her gaze to turn to mine," you know I'm not kidding about how I feel about you yeah?"

"I guess Jax...It's just hard to hear when I can't say the words back."

"I get it Bel, but please will you be my girlfriend?"

She looks at me with uncertainty in her eyes. I want to do something to make her see that I'm sincere. I've always wanted her, even when she was my brother's girlfriend. Jace was an idiot, letting Bella get away, but his stupidity is my gain.

"Bel, please answer me."

"Yes, ok...but I need time to feel the same way, Jax. I don't know if I ever will."

I'm about to reply when her name is called to go in for her ultrasound. She stands up, looking down at me, "Aren't you coming?"

"You want me in the room?"

"Yes, Jax, you're my boyfriend now aren't you?" She stumbles on the word boyfriend and laughing I stand up to follow her down the small hallway.

She climbs up on the table and the technician asks her to lift up her t-shirt.

Her belly is clearly showing now and pulling up a chair beside her I smile wide as the wand is placed over it and the image of our baby appears on the screen.

It's clearly a baby, the technician speaks softly pointing out the heartbeat flickering. Her words are soft, "Well Bella, it appears you're about four months along and all seems to be on track. Would you like to hear the heartbeat?"

We both nod, and the sound of our baby's heartbeat fills the room. It's amazing and my heart swells with love. When Bella came knocking on my door four months ago I never would've dreamt of being at this point with her, just wanting to fuck her but now I want so much more.

~~

With pictures in hand of our baby, we head back to my place.

Bella looks so tired but incredibly beautiful.

Seeing her pregnant makes her even more stunning and I'm aching to be with her to show her that I mean the words I love you.

Once inside she starts stripping like she usually does, "I'm going to have a shower," she says softly taking more clothes off as she heads towards the bathroom. It's definitely a naughty invitation and my daks feel tighter just thinking about her naked in my bathroom.

Reaching the bathroom a minute or so later I find her standing in my double shower completely naked with the water cascading all over her lightly tanned skin.

"Fuck Bella, you're so fucking beautiful," I say, yanking my shirt off and pulling my daks and boxers down with lightning speed.

Stepping into the shower with her, she doesn't say a word instead kisses me hard, wrapping an arm around my neck, the other cupping my chin as she deepens the kiss.

My cock is brushing against her inner thigh, and I grab her leg hoisting her up to hold her over my body.

The tip of my cock teases her entrance, and a little moan escapes her lips against mine.

Letting her go she turns around, pressing her arse against me, turning her head back to kiss me as she teases my cock.

Pulling back she looks at me with lust in her eyes, "Jax fuck me please," she begs.

I don't hesitate, slamming inside her from behind.

She grips me like a vice, rocking her hips back and forth on my length, screaming and moaning so loudly the neighbours two doors down could possibly hear her.

"Jax, fuck....oh....fuck!!" she screams out before kissing me as her body starts shaking, her orgasm building.

Reaching down I tease her clit, breaking the kiss to whisper in her ear, "Come for me Bella, I love when you come for me, baby."

She moans, her body still slamming against mine, the delicious sound of flesh against flesh.

Still, I tease her clit, rubbing it harder as she moans, "Mmm...Jax...fuck...oh fuck I'm coming....fuck!"

Her final release is sudden, her body shaking as she rides it out and I shoot my own load into her, her vice-like grip around my cock milking me hard as I pound into her one last time.

Turning to face me, she kisses me, "Jax that was amazing."

"You're telling me, Bel. I love you so fucking much. And when you fuck me like that you make me wonder."

"Wonder what?"

"How you feel about me? Is sex with him like that?"

"Well, um, no...its um different but I..." I cut her off pressing a kiss to her lips.

"Don't Bel ok?"

"Ok," she replies meekly stepping out of the shower and grabbing a towel.

I watch her for a moment before I step out to grab a towel myself. Hugging her from behind and kissing the side of her head I say softly, "You know your showing babe yeah?"

"Yeah, I know."

"You need to tell Austin and Anni, they both need to know."

"They'll hate me," she replies with a worried tone.

"No, they won't babe, they love you...just tell them yeah?"

"Ok, I guess. Thanks for being there today Jax. It means a lot."

"I wouldn't have missed it, Bel."

Her smile is so sweet then, it melts my heart and I pull her into a hug, kissing her forehead.

"I love you, Bella," I whisper, hearing her sigh into my chest.

I'm not going to stop telling her how I feel until she can tell me the same, until the flicker of her heart beating against mine is a thump like mine is.

Thirty-Seven | Trying It On

Annika

It feels so strange and exciting to be in a bridal
boutique, about to choose a wedding dress.

To be marrying Jairus still feels surreal, a dream come
true. He has a way of making me feel so incredibly
beautiful and has blown my shyness and
inhibitions out of the water.

I love him with all my heart and want to choose a
dress that shows off my body.

Jairus always tells me I have delectable curves.

I fail to see that but take his word for it.

Bella has parked her butt on the antique couch in the
waiting area. I'd told the salesperson I wanted
something with lace that is fitted.

Stepping behind the curtain, a dress hanging up
amongst a couple others catches my eye.

It has a scoop neckline with three quarter lace
sleeves. From under the bust, it flows into a simple
A-line. The lace is scalloped, off-white and I know it's
exactly what I want.

Quickly I undress, down to my seamless nude knickers and strapless push-up bra.

Taking the dress off the hanger, I slide the zip down before stepping into it. Sliding the zip back up against my skin I turn to admire myself in the full-length mirror behind me.

My heart skips a beat, as I slide the curtain open and step out into the waiting area.

Bella takes one look at me, her mouth falling open.

"Oh my god, Anni, you look stunning."

"Really?"

"Yes, dufus. That dress was made for you," she smiles through tears that are dripping down her cheeks.

"Do you think Jai will like it?"

"Of course, it shows off your body."

I laugh, "Yeah my delectable curves."

"You said it, girl," she replies smiling.

The salesperson comes back into the room, "Is this your dress? It looks beautiful on you."

"Are you saying yes to the dress Anni?" Bella asks with cheekiness in her tone.

"Yes, I'm saying yes to the dress!" I beam.

"Fabulous, and will you be looking at any bridesmaid dresses today as well?"

"Yeah, if you're up for it Bel?"

"Ok, I guess."

A hint of a smile curves at the corner of her lips, but
I'm not convinced that she's happy at the prospect of
choosing a dress to wear as my Maid of Honour.
I go to change out of the dress, while Bella goes to
look at the bridesmaid dresses in the other room.

When I find her looking at the dresses ten minutes
later, she's running her hand over a tight-fitting
purple dress with a sad look on her face.
Stepping up next to her I ask, "Bel what's up?"
She looks at me with tears in her eyes, "I um...I won't
be able to wear any of these."
"Why Bel?"
"I um...I need to tell you something..well a couple of
things actually," she confesses, stepping away from
the dress racks to sit down on the couch opposite.

Sitting down next to her I touch her arm lightly,
locking my eyes on hers when I softly say, "You can
tell me anything Bel...has something happened with
Austin?"
"Well, um, yeah kinda," she confesses blushing.

I don't mean my tone, but find myself snapping,

"What Bel? Are you together?"

"No, but god Anni," she pauses, standing up to walk

away.

She turns back to look at me, "I don't want to tell you

here."

I stand up as well, "Ok...come back to mine. We can

chat over coffee. Jai's away at a game."

"Ok...but do you have tea?"

"Yeah I do," I reply smiling and linking my arm with

hers.

We leave then, after I finalise everything for the

dress, putting down a deposit on it.

In the car on the way home, Bella looks across at me

tentatively, " I'm sorry we didn't get to choose

my dress yet."

"It's ok Bel, we've got time," I say smiling at her.

Thankfully it's a short drive and once back at the

penthouse Bella follows me into the elevator.

"God Anni, this place is amazing."

"Yeah, just a little. I can't believe I'm so lucky."

She doesn't reply, following me in and looking

around the kitchen, "So you want coffee or tea?"

"Tea," she replies softly.

I start to prepare it and Bella goes to sit in the sunken lounge, flopping down and sighing like all the worries of the world are on her shoulders.

Thirty-Eight | Secrets Laid Bare
Bella

Anni walks over from the kitchen holding two mugs. I sit up on the sunken lounge as I take my cup of tea from her.

Inhaling the warm, sweet tea I sigh deeply, not even sure where to begin telling Anni all the secrets I'm hiding from her.

She sits down next to me, sipping her coffee, but not saying a word.

After a few sips, she smiles at me, "So Bel, what's bothering you?"

"I don't know where to start," I confess taking the final sip of my tea, before putting the mug on the couch beside me.

Anni lets out a slight laugh as she finishes her coffee.

"Did something happen with you and Austin?"

"Yeah, we've been sleeping together since the party last year and I'm in love with him."

"Oh shit Bel. Have you told him? Maybe he feels the same."

"We both know that's not true Anni. He's still hung up on you and maybe someone else."

"How could there be someone else Bel? If you're sleeping with him?"

"Well, its um...kinda a friends with benefits thing and um...something else happened," I say biting my lip and feeling the blush rise up my cheeks.

"What Bel? You're blushing! You never blush!"

"I can't believe I'm telling you this!"

"What? Telling me what?"

"I had a threesome with him and his mate Kaden."

"Oh my god, Bel! That's so dirty! Was it good?" she screeches before laughing.

"Yeah it was but it was when I realised I was in love with Austin. It made me so damn jealous and I also found out something else."

"Yeah, what's that?"

"I'm pregnant Anni . Possibly with Austin's baby. But it could also be Jax's."

The look on Anni's face is shock but she asks with concern, "Why didn't you tell me sooner?"

"I only just found out, and I thought you'd hate me because I could be pregnant at your wedding."

"No, you won't be Bel... it's the 8th of Dec, you'll have had your baby then if you're keeping it."

"Yeah true, if I'm as far as long as the doctors are telling me. And yes I'm keeping it."

"Yeah, so you really don't know if it's Austins or Jaxons?" she asks, and I shake my head.

"No, and I'm so confused Anni."

"Why? Whose do you want it to be?"

"I don't know...Austin's kinda but Jax is being so sweet to me. I wish I was in love with him instead. It's so messed up Anni. I'm really sorry."

"For what Bel?"

"Falling in love with Austin," I say meekly.

"Why would you be sorry about that Bel?"

"Because...I don't know. He was...is your best friend."

"Yeah..." she muses, "but at the moment you speak to him. I don't."

The look on her face is forlorn and it stabs at my heart.

"Do you miss him?"

"Heaps," she confesses, tears dripping down her cheeks, "I want to tell him I'm engaged but he's gonna be angry at me."

Caz May

I bite down on my lip, wondering if I should tell her
my little slip of telling him already, "I um kinda told
him... I didn't mean to...it just slipped out."
She laughs, "That's ok Bel...its better he knows. I
don't think he'll be coming to the wedding though."
My mouth drops open in shock this time, "You
haven't invited him?"
Shaking her head she replies, "No...Jai told me I
should've but I've already sent the invites."
"Oh Anni," I say reaching out to hug her.
"I'm so glad you're in my life Bel and I can't believe
I'm going to be an Aunty," she trills excitedly.
"You'll be an amazing Aunty Anni, but you'd be an
even better Mum."
"Yeah, but Jai and I aren't ready yet...we just want to
spend some time together and maybe start trying
after we get married," she says with a hint of longing
in her tone.
"Fair enough... I love you, Anni. Thanks for
everything. I'd be lost without you," I confess.
"Aww Bel you'll make me cry," she says sniffing back
tears.

I hug her again, and when she pulls away she pokes
me in the stomach playfully, "So you and Jaxon huh?"

I laugh, "Yeah... I like him, Anni, I mean he's not Aust...but we're good together."

"Are you gonna bring him to the wedding?"

"I guess... I haven't really thought that far ahead," I laugh.

"Well you can if you want, "Anni suggests.

"Thanks...so who am I partnered with anyway?"

Anni blushes, "Um Travis...he's Jai's best friend Bel, so he's his best man."

I let out a squeal, "Oh my god, really? He's literally walking sex."

She laughs at my comment, "But you have a boyfriend now Bella," she jeers at me.

"Yeah," I muse, feeling my core tighten as thoughts of the party a year ago fill my head.

Dancing with Travis at the party made my underwear damp.

I felt him grind against me and his abs were like an ironing board. I've definitely had dirty thoughts about Jairus' best friend and I know I'm in trouble big time.

Thirty-Nine | Tell Him Girl

Bella

About to get in the elevator to leave it opens to a sad looking Blondie who does a double take when he looks at me.

"Hey, sunshine, who knocked you up?"

I give him a slight smile. "Hi, Blondie. And um I don't know," I confess.

"Oh shit. Well, I hope you're ok. Let us know if you need anything. Anni loves you like a sister, so anything you need."

He reaches out to hug me and it feels a little weird hugging him when I've thought for months that he is sex on legs just like his best mate. But it's nothing like hugging Austin, purely platonic like a brotherly hug. Stepping back I softly speak, "Thanks Blondie, that means a lot. You and Anni mean the world to me. I'm so glad she found you Jairus."

He smiles at my use of his actual name, "Aww thanks Bella, I love her so fucking much. Can I tell you a secret?"

"Yeah sure thing Blondie," I giggle.

He leans into my ear to whisper.

"I know Anni has probably told you she doesn't want to get pregnant, but she's been missing her pills."

I step back, my mouth falling open. "Well, maybe I won't be the only one having a baby. I better get going Blondie."

"Ok sunshine," he laughs winking at me as he opens his front door with his swipe card.

His wink suggests that he is going to get up to something dirty with Anni when he walks inside.

I can't help but smile and laugh at the thought.

Pregnancy hormones are also having an effect on my body big time, and anytime sex crosses my mind my body gets a little too excited.I'm never more glad to be going back to Jaxon's.

~~

Getting back to Jax's I find him sitting on the couch, watching TV shirtless with dark blue jeans on.

He looks hot, and I find myself licking my lips as I look at him, sitting on the other end of the couch.

"Hey, you ok?" he says taking in my bedraggled appearance.

"Not really, I told Anni, but i'm worried about telling Austin."

He reaches out to touch my thigh, squeezing it, "You need to tell him Bella...about the baby and us."

"I know...i'll text him now," I reply smiling.

Jumping up from the couch, I run to my bag grabbing out my phone to type a text to Austin.

Bella: We need to talk...when are you free for a chat?

Austin: why you asking that Bel? you technically still live here

Bella: I know...i'm um staying with a friend...are you home Monday night?

Austin: I'm busy all week Bel, I've got a big match coming up and getting in heaps of practice in between shit with uni

Bella: ok well text me when you'll be home...its kinda important

Austin: ok fine

Putting my phone back on the coffee table I sit back down next to Jax, closer this time, leaning into his side. He puts an arm around me, pulling me against his chest.

"So?" he asks kissing my forehead.

"He's being an arsehole. I think he's mad at me."

Jax nods before he replies, "Don't worry about it until you speak to him."

"Yeah, I guess," I mutter looking at Jax whilst I bite down on my lip.

"You are going to tell him yeah?" he asks, trying not to smirk.

"Yeah, but can we just stop talking now."

"Why?"

I lean up to whisper in his ear, "I'm horny, hot stuff."

He laughs, "Hot stuff huh?"

I move, straddling him, grinding against his pelvis as I kiss his neck, teasingly brushing my lips against his skin.

His hips rise into mine, "Fuck Bel, you know how to tease me."

Pulling back I laugh, smirking at him as I pull my t-shirt over my head to expose the lacy sheer black bralette I'm wearing.

He pulls me down for a kiss, moaning as it turns dirty with tongues.

I can feel his growing erection pressing against my aching core.

I continue kissing him, grinding against him more, reaching down between us to undo his jeans.

He gasps, breaking the kiss as I free his cock from his guy front boxers.

Running my hands up and down his length he tips his head back in pleasure.

"God Bel, just like that, sexy."

Laughing I stop and look at him with a smirk on my face, "Sexy huh?" I tease.

"You know you're damn sexy Bella, and with your bump starting to show you're even sexier than ever."

"Oh really? Anything else you find sexy about me Jax? You know my eyes are not in the middle of my chest."

He lets out a deep laugh, reaching up to cup my fuller breasts in his palms, "I might like that your delectable tits are getting bigger."

"Typical male," I laugh, helping him with removing the lacy bralette.

He doesn't let me think or say anything else before taking one hard bud and full mound into his mouth.

I tip my head back, moaning as the pleasure rushes through me straight to my already soaked knickers.

When he stops, not treating the other nipple to the same sweet torture he teases, "Bel, you've soaked your sexy black undies."

"Yeah," I mutter blushing.

"Take them off Bel. I wanna touch you."

Standing up I slip my knickers down my legs, kicking them aside and watching Jax lift his butt up off the couch to push his jeans down his legs to a pile on the floor.

"Come here sexy," he instructs me, his arms outstretched.

Again I straddle him, kissing him as he wraps his hands around my back.

My dripping core is aligned with his cock, and I'd only have to shift a mere centimetre to slide down onto him.

Instead, I break the kiss, my forehead against when I whisper, "Touch me, hot stuff."

Sitting up I see his eyes darken, as his hand slips between us and he slides two fingers into my wet aching need.

"Fuck, Bel. You're so fucking wet, sexy."

He thrusts his fingers in and out, pressing one against my g-spot making me rock my hips as I fuck his fingers hard and fast.

With one finger still inside, he brushes one against my throbbing clit, flicking it and teasing it as I buck against him.

"God Jax...fuck...that...feels...so...so...good!" I scream out in raspy breaths, suddenly shaking as my release hits me and soaks the front of his guy fronts.

Pulling his fingers out, he licks one clean before teasing me, "You made me wet Bel."

"Sorry," I laugh, bending down to kiss him.

He stops my lips pressing to his by putting his other finger to my lips.

I lick it clean, making him moan before he pulls me down to kiss him again. Tasting myself on his lips is making me feel aroused again, and I break the kiss to whisper in his ear, "Jaxon, take me to the bedroom."

"Mmm, sounds like the best idea," he growls standing up and wrapping his arms around me in a tight hug.

His hard dick brushes against the bottom of my baby bump, and as we stumble towards the bedroom kissing I wonder if I could fall for Jaxon, if I could love him outside of the bedroom.

But the moment I think of love, only one person pops into my mind and I hate myself for thinking about Austin whilst kissing Jaxon.

Forty | Truths Comes Out

I'm gunning the ute down Bridge Road so fast my heart is pounding and hearing sirens approaching I'm sure it's cops coming to pull me over.

My mind is all over the place, seeing Anni again and her carrying a wedding dress.

It hurts like hell and my emotions hit me hard again. There is a small part of my heart that does still love her and even though I've acted on my attraction to Kaden, and Bella I still feel a pang of attraction to Anni as well.

Plus I'm also developing feelings for Dana, that scare the absolute shit out of me as I've not even kissed her yet, but I just want to be around her.

Arriving home fifteen minutes later, thankfully not having been pulled over by the cops that drove past me I park the ute and text Bella as I head inside.

Austin: Bel, come over now, need to chat

Bella: fine Aust, be there when I finish work at like five

Glancing at the clock I see it's only three-thirty, so I head to the fridge to grab a beer before I sprawl out on the couch to lose myself in a game of Super Mario Odyssey.
The time thankfully passes quickly, despite my racing thoughts.

When Bella knocks on the door at almost exactly five I answer, leaning against the door frame as I look her up and down.
Her belly is really round, a small bump that wasn't there the last time I saw her a couple months ago.
It's obvious she's pregnant.

"Bel, fuck why didn't you tell me?"
She pushes me inside and I close the door behind us.
"Because I don't know whether it's yours Aust," she says shaking her head.
I know my mouth falls open in shock, "So you slept with someone else?" I ask, kind of hoping she says yes and I'm off the hook.
"Yes, Jaxon," she replies blushing but not meeting my eyes.

"Seriously Bella? Your ex's brother?"

"Yes..we're together now," she informs me, like its supposed to make what she's doing the right choice.

"God Bel I can't believe you...that's wrong even for you."

"Talk about yourself Austin...fucking with your best guy mates feelings is worse," she chastises me, hitting me where it hurts with her words.

It almost feels like she's kneed me in the balls when mentioning Kaden.

"Yeah I know ok....we've barely spoken and I miss my mate...but we need some space."

"Yeah as do we Austin...so I'm staying at Jax's," she tells me with anger in her tone.

"Fine...oh and you were right about Anni and Jairus getting married," I tell her, my heart constricting when I say his name.

"You should contact her....she misses you and wants you there Austin."

"I don't have her number, Bella."

"I'll text it to you," she says like it's the most simple thing in the world and all will be forgiven from one simple exchange of numbers.

Anni has made it clear she wants nothing to do with me. I'd fucked that up and I don't want to fuck things

up even more with Bella. It seems as though she is
pushing me away as well.

"Ok, thanks...so no hard feelings between us Bel?" I
ask, playfully poking the top of her bump.
She shakes her head, blushing, "No Aust...I love you,"
she admits looking at the floor.
I gape, "Um...what Bel?" I ask, even though I heard
her words exactly.
"Not like that dufus," she snaps before reaching out
and hugging me, "I gotta go, but text Anni ok?"
She takes a step back when I reply, "I will...bye Bel."

She turns towards the door, opening it and waving
back at me as she leaves.
Closing it behind her I can't help but wonder if she
does mean her words.
The last couple of times we slept together left a
strange feeling in the pit of my stomach, confusing
me as her kisses had changed.
They seemed more loving, sweet and not lustful.
The more I thought about it the sex we had after the
threesome was the kinda sex you had with someone
you loved, slow and sweet, not just fucking like horny
rabbits.
I really had fucked up everything with Kaden too.

I know I don't have romantic feelings for him, but I love being with him in a physical sense.

Getting off with a guy is intense in an erotic way that is so different than with a girl and I secretly love the fact I can cum inside his arse or all over his body without consequence.

Bella isn't sure whether her baby is mine, but I have my suspicions.

We'd had way too much unprotected sex and I'm angry at myself now, as I'd not thought of the consequences when the lust was evident between us.

Picking up my phone from the coffee table I send Kaden a text.

Austin: Kaden I miss you mate...we need to talk
Kaden: yeah ok...a drink after boxing on wednesday?
Austin: sounds ripper :)

Putting my phone back down I lay back on the couch again, losing myself in my Mario game to escape from the truth that is plaguing my mind.

I'm most likely having a kid, I've lost my best friend, my best guy mate is in love with me, whilst I'm still in love with a girl I'll never have and I'm having confusing feelings towards another girl who won't let me in.

The truth fucking sucks.

Forty-One | Hearts Actually Shatter
Kaden

After a tough boxing session in which I've had to completely ignore Austin to not sport a hard on I follow him to the locker room.

He's pulling on jeans, and a crisp white shirt that he shrugs a dark brown leather jacket over.
"Hey Aust, nice get-up. Give me a minute and we can head out yeah?"
"No worries," he replies grabbing out his phone and texting someone, most likely Dana, with a smirk on his face.

I pull on my white jeans, and a blue shirt with flamingos on it. It's a risky outfit to wear to the pub, but it looks good on me, accentuating my arse and package.
My heart is still Austin's but I'm kinda hoping to pick up anyone willing for the night to forget about how insanely in love with my best mate I actually am.

He looks up at me, his eyes darkening as he takes in
my outfit.

He probably doesn't mean to but licks his lips, his
gaze wandering over my body.

"Mmm, Kad, hot outfit man."

"Thanks, Aust, you look pretty ripper yourself. Ready
to get tanked?"

"Yeah, I need a couple of stiff ones," he replies
laughing, sending blood rushing to the front of my
jeans as we head out.

Ten minutes later, only a short walk from boxing we
enter the pub.

Sauntering up to the bar I order a bourbon on the
rocks for both of us, paying for them and handing
one to Austin.

He clinks his glass against mine, downing it so quickly
I've barely had a chance to sip mine before he's
signalling for another to the bartender.

Another drink is slid down to him, and he pays before
we move away to find a spot to sit for a bit.

Sliding into a booth at the back, he asks, "Are you ok,
Kad?"

"Yeah, Aust...I just needed some space, but
I've missed you."

"I'm sorry Kad... I really liked being with you but I..."

I cut him off, my heart shattering when I say the words, "You're falling for Dana yeah?"

"I don't know...I really like her, but we've only been out like once," he replies sipping his bourbon and running a finger along the rim of the glass as he's thinking about what else to say.

"And? How was the date?" I ask not sure if I really want to know all the details.

Thinking about him being with someone else is torture. Sitting across from him now I just want to kiss him, head out of the pub and take him back to mine to show him the new toy I'd picked up a couple of weeks ago after the threesome.

I've been watching countless porn videos using double ended dildos and now looking at Austin sipping his bourbon across the table from me I'm cracking a fat thinking about using it with him as we kiss and wank until we both come.

His voice breaks my wicked thoughts, thankfully sending my hard on south, "Amazing...but she was a little frigid...wouldn't let me kiss her."

"Oh shit man, she doesn't seem like the type."

"I know right, but I don't know, things are different with us and I'm kinda glad I didn't kiss her yet."

"But you want to?"

"Fuck yeah, she's gorgeous. It's like forbidden fruit."

"Mmm, yeah, I get you," I moan looking at him and the lust that darkens his eyes when he looks away towards the doors.

"Speaking of," he laughs nodding his head towards the entrance.

"She's here? Did you text her?"

"I might have," he replies blushing.

Dana walks over to the table, meekly bending over to kiss Austin on the cheek, "Hey stud."

"Hey gorgeous," he replies standing up and hugging her.

"Are you ready to go to Rivera?" she asks him, looking at me like I've got something she clearly doesn't want or maybe does want, as though Austin is mine.

"Sure gorgeous," Austin replies, waving back at me, "Catch ya at boxing Kad," he says loudly as she pulls him out of the pub with a cheeky grin on her face. Undoubtedly Austin is going to hook up with her tonight.

I can't get the image of them pashing on the dance-floor at Rivera out of my head. I want it so badly to be me still able to pash him, but hearts only shatter when you fall in love with your best friend.

Mine has actually shattered, and downing the last of my bourbon I leave the pub, no longer in the mood to hook up.

My night is going to end with a dildo in my arse as I wank hard thinking about putting my shattered heart back together.

Forty-Two | Dance Floor Liaisons

Dana

Dragging Austin out of the pub, my heart is pounding and my head spinning with a mix of emotions.

There is so much I want to say to him, starting with questioning the tension between him and the guy we'd just left alone in the pub.

He hasn't told me much about his past relationships, except for falling for Annika and something that happened with some friends that really confused him sexually.

I've briefly mentioned Ben, and about finding out he was cheating on me with another teacher at his school called Sara.

Austin questioned me, and I felt like karma was giving me a kick up the butt when I found out that Sara was Jairus' ex-girlfriend and she'd been cheating on him with Ben.

Austin knew I'd thrown myself at Travis, sleeping with him and anyone else willing until I got the courage to take Austin's number.

I remember being at the game with him last year, and my stomach still flip-flops when I think about him looking at me out of the corner of his eyes.

I've never admitted it, but I've had a crush on Austin since then and when I like someone more than just physically, when I feel like I have a connection with someone that is beyond physical I shut down, becoming a shy church mouse.

Austin is now giving me that same look as we head down Bridge road, holding hands.

"You ok, Dan?" He asks smiling at me.

"Yeah I'm fine" I lie clenching my teeth together as I follow him into Rivera.

Smirking at me he leads me straight onto the dance floor, pulling me close against his body when he leans in to whisper in my ear, "Let go gorgeous."

His breath is warm, his tone husky and I feel my knickers dampen.

Austin gets to me without even trying, his words, his body so close to mine is again making my head spin.

Taking in a deep breath I let him wrap his arms around my waist, as I wrap mine around his neck.

He moves my hips, rubbing my pelvis against his erection.

"Dan, please..." he moans.

I can barely hear him above the music pumping around us, but I can see his eyes darkening as they linger on my face, my lips.

My breath hitches, he's looking at my lips, leaning in about to kiss me but I can't let him, not yet.

I cough, untangling my arms around his neck and freeing myself from his arms around me as I run out of the club without even looking back.

I know he'll follow me out, and I feel his presence behind me only a metre or so away from Rivera.

He stops me from rushing away, grabbing my arm and asking, "What's wrong Dan?"

I sigh, "That guy from earlier? That was him yeah? The guy you fucked?"

The word 'fucked' is foreign on my tongue, a poisonous word I hate associating with sex outside of the bedroom.

"Yeah, but there's nothing going on between us. We're just friends," Austin says, his lips turning up at the corner making my heart sink with the possibility that he's lying to me.

"You seemed pretty cozy," I suggest biting down on my lip as I look up at him to search his eyes for some hope that I'm not going to be ditched again.

"Dan I promise there is nothing going on between Kaden and me...I wanna be with you."

Those words make me smile and I reply, still a little trepidatious "I wanna be with you too Aust...but I'm scared."

"Of what?" He asks, brushing his fingers against my cheek.

"Of how much I wanna be with you..." I confess, snapping my mouth shut before I say too much.

Austin smiles, making my insides melt and my knickers dampen even more, making them feel like they've disintegrated.

"I get you, Dan, ok...I don't wanna rush things with you," he says sweetly before kissing my forehead, "I like you, Dana."

I love you Austin

"I like like you, Austin," I say meekly, hoping the look on his face doesn't mean I've just said the words in my head instead.

He laughs as he takes my hand and laces our fingers together. The sweet touch as we walk to his Ute sends a tingle running up my arm that confirms my earlier admission to myself.

I'm not just falling in love with him but I am in love with Austin Belvinz and after Ben, I'm afraid of getting my heart broken.

Forty-Three | Eyes Watching On

Dana is dragging me into Marvel stadium, and I can't wipe the obvious disgust from my face.

Being at one of Jairus' games is the last place I want to be.

"Dan, do we really have to go to his game?" I ask, squeezing her hand that I'm clutching onto for dear life.

"Yes Aust, I'm in the cheer squad, and today we're a couple girls down."

"I get that gorgeous, but what if Annika's here? She probably comes to all his games."

"Anni isn't here. She told me she can't make it today, something about a doctor's appointment."

I glare at her, questioning her, but when she doesn't reply I decide better than to push it.

Things are good with us, and I don't want to pick a fight because of my own insecurities.

Sitting down in the stands behind the goals ten minutes later, I look around, feeling a little calmer when I realise Annika is nowhere to be found.

The players are out on the field warming up and catching Jairus' eye I turn away, looking anywhere but at him. It feels weird watching him play.

Dana is fussing about with the other cheer squad members, barking directions to them and watching others out on the field setting up the banner for the team to run through.

I feel like a fish out of water at a game, and try to focus on Dana when she sits down beside me for a moments breather.

The start of the game is a blur, Richmond clearly dominating the scoreboard and I watch Dana cheering for Jairus and Travis.

Feigning interest I try to join in but I can't call out 'Jai the man' as I imagine Annika screaming it out whilst their fucking.

Hearing Dana scream it out, feels like a stab in the guts and I wish I'd brought headphones with me to block the world out.

Half time thankfully comes quicker than I'm expecting but Dana is quiet, fidgeting in her seat and not focusing on anything in particular.

"Dan is something wrong?" I ask, touching her arm, running my fingers up and down her bare arm.

She turns to look at me when she replies
unconvincingly, "No...why?"

I don't directly answer her question, instead ask, "Do
you still like him?"

She gives me a questionable look, again replying with
the same words as though she's confused, "No why?"

This time I know I need to try and be a bit more
specific with what I'm asking. I don't ask a
question, instead state with a hint of anger, "He's
been practically eye fucking you all game."

She laughs, not getting that I'm annoyed, "Who
Aust?"

"Travis," I snap.

Again she laughs, and her answer irritates me, "He
always does that."

"Yeah?" I ask when she looks at me blushing.

"Yeah, don't worry about it."

Her words grate me, how could I not worry about it?
I know about their past together and he doesn't
seem like the type of guy who'd give a shit if
someone is taken.

"I don't like it Dana," I inform her, using her full name
to hopefully give her the sense that I'm upset.

"Why? It doesn't mean anything Aust."

"I don't like it....because..." I stammer, hoping it's the right time to say the next words as we've not had that conversation, "because you're my girlfriend Dana."

She glares at me, her eyes darkening, her cheeks flushing, "Your girlfriend?"

"Yes Dana....my girlfriend."

"But we've...we've never even kissed," she stammers, biting down on her luscious pink lips.

"And who's fault is that?" I question her, about to probe her more, instead biting down on my lip too.

She looks at me oddly, her chest hitching as she thinks about my words.

Forty-Four | Affectionate Sideline Games

Dana

Austin is gawking at me, biting his lip between his teeth like he's holding back from saying something.

I feel foolish, frustrated with myself that I haven't let him kiss me when it's clear he wants to.

Meekly I reply, "It's mine."

"Dana don't say that," he bleats, in a sweet calming way that makes my heart pound.

"But it is Austin... I've been pushing you away... I'm sorry."

He steps closer to me, our bodies not quite touching.

With the back of his hand, he caresses my cheek, "Don't be."

I smile, gazing straight into his eyes, forgetting we are in the middle of Marvel Stadium when he murmurs my name, wetting his lips with his tongue.

I grab his hand squeezing it as I lean forward pressing my lips against his in a quick sweet kiss.

Pulling back I feel my cheeks flush and turn away from his eyes that won't leave mine.

He tries to pull me back for another kiss, "Dan?"

I turn back to his gaze, hoping my cheeks are still not heated, "What?" I snap.

"Are you ok?" he asks, touching my arm lightly, sending tingles rushing through my body.

I want to give in, to kiss him properly, but I feel like every single person in the stadium is watching on.

"Um yeah..can we just watch the rest of the game? And forget that kiss?"

He doesn't reply, instead pulls me against his side.

I squirm a little but only because it feels so nice.

There's something so different about being in Austin's arms compared to Travis's and even Ben's.

I'm confused and kind of surprised that he doesn't try to kiss me again, didn't try to take the kiss further.

For a moment, I wonder if he does want me as much as he says, if he really means that he wants me to be his girlfriend.

We sit down when the siren sounds and his arm is still around me, trying to pull me closer even with the gap in the seat between us.

I want nothing more than to kiss him again but the game has started again and he seems distracted, not sure where to look. He presses a kiss to my cheek, before standing up and grabbing my hand.

"Dan, I'm going to go, I...I...can't be here anymore."
I stand up, not saying anything. He wraps his arms around me in a warm hug.
"Ok, are we good?" I ask warily.
"Yes Dana, we're good. I'll talk to you later."
"Ok," I reply, stretching up on my tiptoes to kiss him on the cheek before he walks out of the row of seats, excusing himself as he brushes past people's knees.

I'm not sure whether to believe his words that everything is good between us.
After the stupid peck of a kiss, he's walking away from me with barely an explanation.
My heart is shattering in my chest and I'm torn between staying at the game and running after him.

I want Austin, I want to show him that I'm falling for him, but I'm afraid, still, that he's not feeling the same as me and I curse myself turning back to the field giving Travis a wink when he bumps into the barrier in front of me.

Forty-Five | Crashing Down Hard

Vairus

The siren going off for the beginning of the third
quarter sounds like a freight train in my head.
My neck feels stiff, achy and for a moment I wonder
where in the world I am.
After ball up, the lights of the ground seem brighter
than before when I look up trying to focus on
marking the ball.
Jumping up to grab the ball my knees ache and I feel
as though I have no strength in my legs at all.
I hear everything, all the words around me, telling
me to kick the ball but I know as soon as it leaves my
foot and I fall down to the ground suddenly feeling
an overwhelming sense of confusion that it's a clear
miss.
Travis extends a hand to help me up but I feel pain in
my ankle, a dull throbbing ache in the joint.
"You good mate?" Travis asks as he pulls me up.
"Yeah um Nah I um," I mutter confusedly.

Travis nods to the umpire who calls play on and the game continues around me for about ten minutes.

I feel a little drowsy, but shake my head trying to focus on what is going on around the ground when I hear Travis calling out to me, "Jai, mark it mate!"

Again I go to mark the ball but dizziness fills my head. I jump up to grab the ball, but my vision is blurry, causing me to miss the mark and I fall down from shoulder height of the other player to the ground. I know the impact is going to be hard, and bracing myself I close my eyes, crashing down, landing on my ankle.

It's underneath me and I hear and feel it crack before my head hits the ground and my surrounds go black.

Forty-Six | Not Ready Yet

Annika

My phone buzzes in my pocket the moment I walk out of the doctors.

My heart falls to the ground, seeing the words 'Epworth Hospital' on my flashing screen.

I answer as calmly as I can, "Hello Annika Mathers speaking."

"Hello Ms Mathers, this is Madelyn from the Epworth, in regards to you being listed as an emergency contact for a Mr Jairus Brooks."

I swallow the lump in my throat, shuffling towards the car, trying to not drop my phone as I frantically search through my handbag for my keys.

"Yes, he's my fiancee."

Her tone is cold when she replies, "He has been admitted for Concussion, but due to his unconscious state upon arrival and a report from some teammates, he has been put into a medically induced coma."

Reaching the car, hearing her words in my ear my heartbeat rises in panic, "A coma? What for?"

"I cannot discuss the details over the phone."

"Um...um...ok I'll be there in twenty minutes."

I don't let her respond, I don't want to hear her cold tone as though she has no empathy and hasn't completely shattered my heart.

I've just received amazing news and horrible news in the space of twenty minutes.

Thankfully, the trip from the doctors to the Epworth only takes fifteen minutes and I easily find a park. Rushing inside the hospital I race straight up to the desk, asking breathlessly, "Jairus Brooks' room?"

She looks at me scornfully, a non-verbal warning of some kind that confuses me.

Sighing I bleat out, "Please, just let me see him."

"He's in room seven Ms Mathers. There is a young man waiting outside in the corridor who came in earlier and says he knows you. The doctor will be in shortly to let you know the details of Mr Brooks' condition."

"Thank you," I mutter, rushing down the hallway.

My heart is pounding, wondering who the young man is, but also because my anxiety is rising.

I can't lose Jairus, he is my everything, has given me everything and my love for him grows every day.

Rounding the corridor outside room seven, in the small waiting area I panic, an odd rush of emotions overwhelming me when I see the figure sitting on the hard plastic chairs.

He appears to be in a world of his own, and I'm not sure if I want to approach him or just go straight in to see Jairus.

Stepping up to the door he makes my decision for me, standing up and touching my arm lightly.

"Hi Anni," he says softly, shuffling his feet on the floor.

"Um, hi Austin. How did you know he...I was coming here?"

He gives me a sheepish grin, "I was at the game with Dana. He went down just as I was leaving and I...I...rushed straight here...I..."

There's an odd sparkle in his eyes, but also a worried concerned look that makes my anxiety skyrocket, "Dana? You were at a game?"

"Yeah we've been seeing each other for month or so ago and we um.."

I'm worried for Jairus, but seeing Austin again, clearly struggling with a whirlwind of emotions is tugging at my heart. I've missed him, my best friend, so much it hurts, like an ache deep in my chest.

"Tell me Austin," I beg sweetly.

"We um...nothing..." he mutters, gesturing towards the door of Jairus' room.

As I open it and he follows me in, I look at him for a moment, not sure what to say, "Oh um ok she hasn't told me anything."

It's awkward, neither of us knowing what to say after nearly a year of not speaking to each other.

We both look down at Jairus in the bed for a moment. He has wires connected to a heart monitor and a drip. His right foot hangs out of the bed and he has a plaster cast on his foot to halfway up his calf.

I whimper, seeing my gorgeous fiancee', again in a hospital bed.

Austin takes a big gulp in, taking my hand in his, running his thumb over my palm when he speaks softly, "Yeah I um...nevermind...I um...really miss you Anni."

I look across at him, squeezing his hand, "I know Austin, I miss you too but I don't know if I'm ready to be friends again."

"I get that Anni, but I'm here for you especially now." He nods towards Jairus.

"Thanks....I'm just really scared I'm going to lose him."

"You won't Anni....he loves you so much...he'll pull through. I know he will."

"I hope so...I can't live without him and I..."
His gaze locks on mine, and I know he can see the distress in my eyes when he pulls me into a hug.

It feels like coming home, having Austin hug me, like hugging family. Tears start to drip down my cheeks, and I sniff them back pulling back from Austin's hug. Looking at him I try to open my mouth to speak, but only whimpered sobs come out.

"What Anni? Why are you crying, babe?"
"I...I...just found out I'm pregnant....that's why I wasn't at the game today and I didn't even get a chance to tell him before this happened," I slowly tell him between sobs.
"Oh, Anni...that's amazing! Congratulations!" he beams, a wide smile crossing his face which surprises

me considering our history and the possibility of
Bella being pregnant with his child as well.

"Thanks...and yeah it is amazing but if I lose Jai I'll be
a single mum...and..." I draw out, before bursting into
uncontrollable tears.

Austin wipes them away from my cheeks with his
thumb, "Don't cry babe."

"But Austin, I'm scared."

"I know babe, but it will be ok. I'm going to go..but
contact me please if you need anything and tell him
your amazing news...sit with him and tell him
everything..you know he can hear you."

"Thanks, Austin..." I mutter through my tears.

He kisses my cheek softly, "We should catch up for a
coffee?"

I smile slightly, "Ok I'll text you..." I inform him.

He looks at me oddly and I laugh, "Yes Austin, I still
have your number."

"Sweet...I'll talk to you soon," he replies, turning to
leave. He waves at me as he exits the room, blowing
me a kiss with a cheeky grin on his face.

I really want my cheeky best friend back in my life, to
share my child's life with and to stop the ache in my
chest from missing him.

I pull a chair up to the side of the bed, kissing Jairus'
forehead and cheek.

Holding his hand, I start to speak, "Hey baby,
I...I...um...love you....and I...I...um..."

I sigh, feeling stupid for talking to him when he's not
awake.

His heartbeat on the screen rises a little though like
he's responding to hearing my voice.

"I was right baby...the doctor confirmed I'm
pregnant."

His heartbeat rises again, and the doctor walks into
the room holding a chart.

"Hello, Ms Mathers yes?"

"Yes, I'm his fiancee'."

"Well, Ms Mathers, your fiancee' had a fall, landing
on his ankle which is badly fractured. He suffered a
mild concussion and was unconscious when leaving
the ground. The teams medical staff informed us of
some other symptoms he's been experiencing
recently also."

"Oh, what symptoms?" I ask standing up, still holding
Jai's hand in mine.

"Are you aware of him complaining of aching joints,
sensitivity to light, drowsiness or confusion?"

"Well he...um...he did tell me last week that his
knees and ankles were especially sore and he'd been

complaining of a headache here and there. But I just thought he wasn't doing his physio exercises enough. Is there something else wrong?" I ask hesitantly with my heart hammering in my chest.

"We've taken blood, and are awaiting results."

"So why the medically induced coma then? Surely his condition is not that serious?"

"It's precautionary Ms Mathers. Currently, he needs rest, as we are suspecting some kind of infection, but until the blood test result comes back we aren't sure."

"Infection? What kinda of infection?"

He looks down at the chart in his hand, and I wish for a moment that Doctor Thompson was in. He'd keep me calm, not leave me in the dark and creep me out with medical terminology. The nurse in me wants to be told straight out what is wrong with Jai, not have some doctor pussyfoot around telling me about his condition.

"We're suspecting he may have Meningitis."

My mouth falls to the floor in shock, "I'm sorry what?"

"Meningitis, Ms Mathers," he informs me as though I'm a completely clueless idiot.

"I heard what you said, but I'm shocked and angry at myself for not seeing the signs."

"They can come on quite quickly, and are not something loved ones generally think out of the ordinary as they are often similar to the flu."

"I get that Doctor, but I'm training to be a nurse, so I should have known something was up."

"As I said, loved ones sometimes don't recognise symptoms. We will know more when we get the blood test results, later this evening."

"Ok, I guess. Will he be given antibiotics?"

"Yes, we believe it may be viral but he will be given I V antibiotics this evening when doctor Thompson arrives for duty."

"Ok, thank you," I reply, inwardly smiling at the thought of Doctor Thompson starting soon.

When the doctor leaves the room I sit back down in the chair, looking at my gorgeous fiancée.

Closing my eyes, I say a little thank you pray that he isn't facing something more serious.

Viral meningitis isn't common, but it's curable and other than the broken ankle needing extra physio he will be fine.

Everything always has a way of working out.

Forty-Seven | Eyes Glued Shut

Jairus

The scrape of a chair being pulled up against the side of the bed is grating. Voices have drifted into my head, but all I can focus on is Anni's melodic comforting voice. She seems genuinely concerned, worried and sitting down beside the bed I feel her grab my hand in hers.

Her soft wet lips kiss first my forehead and then my cheek. It's comforting knowing she's there.

As she holds my hand she talks to me, mumbling. The words are hard to focus on, but I can feel her hand gently squeezing mine.

One word that I hear loud and clear like she's in my head is 'pregnant'.

It makes my heart pounds hearing the confirmation coming from her lips. She'd been over a month late on her period but didn't want to take a test because when she'd been late before a test had always been negative and her period would start.

It was difficult seeing her so upset, so I let it be, encouraging her to go to the doctor when she became unwell.

I should have told her more about my symptoms but I didn't want to worry her unnecessarily.

Desperately I want to open my eyes to tell her how excited I am but I can't. They feel glued shut and it makes me feel panicked.

Again my heartbeat rises, even more so when someone else enters the room.

Again I hear voices, saying words describing my symptoms over the past couple of months.

I don't know what the person is talking about.

It sounds scary, so I tune out his words focusing on Anni instead.

I feel her squeeze my hand again, and try to tell myself to squeeze it back, but my whole body feels paralysed, trapped.

I want to move, I want to scream, but I can't and it's agonisingly terrifying.

The door closes again, and I can tell Anni has sat back down in the chair.

I sense she's looking at me, and all I want to do is open my eyes to look at her gorgeous face, to kiss her and to take satisfaction in celebrating our good news with her, but my eyes are glued shut.

Forty-Eight | Always Only You

Jairus

Opening my eyes feels so surreal. Time has ceased to exist, shut inside myself for god knows how long.

The first thing I see the moment I open my eyes is my gorgeous fiancé sitting by the bed.

She has sleep in the corner of her eyes, smudged mascara and her luscious hair is falling out of a messy ponytail.

A smile on her lips, she coos softly at me, "Hey baby, I missed you."

"Mmm...I missed you to sweetheart, so much. What day is it?"

"Tuesday baby."

"Only Tuesday? Feels like forever."

"Yeah I know, so um..."

I laugh at her, smirking and teasing her, "Got something to tell me, sweetheart?"

"Yeah...I'm pregnant baby," she announces with the biggest grin on her face.

She leans over the bed, her lips just a breath from mine.

"I know sweetheart, I heard you. And fuck I'm so excited. I love you, Annika."

She kisses me quickly, her lips on mine searing even though the contact is quick.

"I love you to Jairus. I'm so glad you're okay."

"You can't get rid of me that easily sweetheart," I laugh.

She slaps my arm playfully, "Haha, not funny Jai! I was so scared, but luckily your results came back as viral meningitis, not bacterial."

"That's all gobbly gook to me, sweetheart."

"Sorry baby, the bacterial kind is worse."

"Ok, well I'm sure I'll be fine with my nurse Anni to look after me at home."

Again she presses a kiss to my lips, so brief I murmur when she breaks it, wanting so much more but knowing the hospital isn't the place.

Standing up she says, "I'll go see if I can find Doctor Thompson so we can organise your discharge. I need to kiss you properly, so bad baby."

I moan, licking my lips as she leaves the room.

I'll never get sick of kissing her, never tire of gazing at her beauty and Annika is the most beautiful when she isn't trying to be, just like she is now from being by my bedside for a couple days.

~~

Thankfully, by the end of the day and the fact Annika is a soon to be nurse means they allow me to leave the hospital earlier than a normal patient would have been allowed.

Stepping into the elevator to the basement carpark of the hospital Anni holds the doors open whilst I hobble in with my crutches.
Leaning against the railing, I speak softly, "Thanks, sweetheart. What would I do without you?"
"You'd still be stuck in a hospital bed, baby."
"That's true, I think I'd much rather being stuck in bed at home with my nurse Anni."

With her help I manage to lean against the rail, pressing my arse against it and holding my ankle up off the floor.
She steps in front of me, after pressing the basement button and pins me in place.
"I love you Jairus, I don't want to ever be without you," she says softly, with her forehead against mine. Her breath is warm, and it makes my lips tingle.

"I love you to Annika. And I'm not going anywhere, but home to bed with you," I tease her sweetly, taking her lips to mine in a demanding kiss.

She murmurs, deepening the kiss with her tongue licking my lips but drawing her tongue back in before I can lace our them together.

It makes my cock rise to attention in my already too tight footy shorts.

Pulling back, I nod towards my crotch and jeer, "Sweetheart, do you see what you did to me?"

"Sorry baby," she laughs when the doors slide open.

She helps me out, thanking the old couple who keep the door open for us. At the car, she helps me in, before throwing my crutches in the backseat.

Once out on the street, she indicates to head home and asks me, "So baby, is there anything special you want to help you recover?"

I murmur, licking my lips thinking back to last time I had a concussion and she looked after me.

Seeing her in the hot nurse outfit is forever burned into my memory, but I definitely wouldn't mind seeing it in person again.

We'd almost had sex that first time she wore it, and this time I can think of nothing else I want more.

"Hmm, sweetheart, I was thinking you could wear your hot nurse outfit again, and actually ride my cock this time."

"Oh really?" she jeers, "I don't know if it will fit me. If you haven't noticed I'm a bit bloated."

"You're not fat sweetheart. Our baby is growing inside you," I say, reaching over and slipping my hand under her t-shirt.

"Jai, that tickles," she screeches squirming a little in her seat as she turns the car into the underground carpark.

"Sorry, sweetheart. Let's get upstairs yeah?"

She doesn't reply as she parks the car in her spot. Jumping out she gets out the crutches before opening my door and helping me stand up.

We hobble to the elevator, and she helps me in, pressing a finger to my lips.

"Uhuh baby, wait until we get upstairs," she taunts, making me laugh.

We usually share a kiss in the elevator but we've already had one today and the ground level button is lit up which means company is sure to join us on the way to our level thirteen penthouse.

After getting inside Anni helps me undress out of my footy clothes. It's beyond awkward getting them over my cast so I leave my boxers on and pull her down on top of me, my head hitting the pillows with a thump. Smashing a kiss to her lips, she moans deeply, finally letting me in to kiss her properly, a hot heated kiss that makes my cock ache.

I really want to fuck her in the hot nurse outfit but don't want to let her go.

I also know that my naughty Anni is quite possibly wearing a g-string under her trackie daks.

She'd bought a couple more since we'd gotten together, my favourite a black barely there one with elastic at the side, a small triangle of fabric at the front.

When I'd found her wearing it under her trackies a couple of months ago, I teased her, asking her why she'd wear a g-string under trackies and her response was dirty and innocent at the same time; she loves the feeling of the fleece on her bare arse.

Kissing me more, she grinds against me and breathless I break the kiss eager to know if she is wearing that g-string.

Hooking my fingers in the elastic of her trackies, I ask with a smirk, "Sweetheart, are you wearing that hot black g under these?"

Her cheeks flush, telling me her answer before she hisses a soft 'yes'.

"Mmm, sweetheart, can I see?" I taunt, pushing the trackies over her arse cheeks and cupping them in my palms. She lifts her body up a bit and helps me push the trackies to her ankles.

Kissing me again she kicks them off, her pelvis and the barely-there fabric now meeting the bulge in my boxers.

When she breaks the kiss, she lifts her t-shirt over her head and I smile at her, gazing at the roundness of her belly with our baby growing inside her.

I don't even take off my boxers, partly because getting them off over my cast is going to be a challenge and partly because I just want to fuck Anni right that very second.

So instead of taking them off I poke my cock out through the fly front hole.

I'm as hard as steel and hiss when Anni grabs my cock in her dainty hand.

"Mmm, sweetheart, I wanna fuck you so bad right now," I tease, reaching between her legs to run a finger over her slit.

She's soaking wet and I bite my lip, just thinking about tasting her is making my cock even harder.

Putting my finger in my mouth I lick it clean, moaning and watching the expression on her face.

Her eyes darken, she smirks and moves the barely-there fabric of her G-string aside.

She lets out a hot as fuck moan, almost a scream of pleasure as she slides straight onto my hard cock.

She rides my cock then, taking me inside her slick wetness, deep, hard and fast.

I pull her down for a kiss, wrapping my arms around her back so she can't move when I sneakily undo her bra clasp.

It falls down her arms, between us when I break the kiss to survey her beautiful body as she fucks me.

"Mmm fuck your beautiful Annika...god being inside you is so fucking amazing, sweetheart."

She smiles wide, pushing her body down hard on my cock, "God Jai baby...having you inside me fuck... I could ride your cock all day, baby."

"Mmm...fuck Anni, so deep sweetheart....tell me what it feels like having my cock buried inside you?" I taunt seductively.

"Fucking awesome Jai!" she bellows, rocking up and down on my cock so hard I can feel it hitting her walls.

"Fuck...oh fuck," she screams in pleasure, pounding down harder again, pushing my cock inside her, deeper than ever.

She leans down to kiss me, a kiss that is teasing hot and demanding. Her tongue darts out, licking my lips.

Her pleasure is increasing, her pace furious, bringing her ever closer to her climax.

Watching her riding my cock with such abandonment is by far the most beautiful sight ever.

She bites my lips as she comes, rocking her pelvis as the shiver and wave of her climax takes over.

Still with my cock buried inside, her body shakes, her climax so intense it makes me explode inside her, my cock pulsating as I fill her with my hot release.

She rolls off to lay next to me, running a finger up and down my abs, "Woah, baby I've never come like that before," she tells me with a delicious smirk on her face that makes me feel like taking her again to make her come again.

"Me either sweetheart, I think I'm going to love having a pregnant fiancee," I laugh, winking at her.

"Mmm yeah...." she murmurs as she nuzzles into my side.

Gently I stroke her hair, pressing a kiss to her forehead, "I love you, Annika Brooks, it's always only been you for me."

She laughs sweetly, "That's not my name yet, but I love the sound of it and I love you Jairus Brooks."

I kiss her softly, loving the rush of warmth and the tingle that races through my body.

Murmuring I deepen the kiss, thinking about how much I love her. I can't wait to make her my wife and to meet our baby.

Protectively I place a hand over her belly, closing my eyes and listening to her breathing as I drift into sleep.

Forty-Nine I Don't Say Goodbye

I'd arrived early in the city to meet Anni for a coffee, and stopped in at Platypus to buy the new Converse shoes I'd been eyeing off for months. They'd cost two hundred bucks, all my winnings from my last boxing match but so worth it.

Carrying the bag proudly I walk into the Gloria Jeans on Elizabeth street, looking around for Anni and wondering if I should order for her when she's not here yet.

She always has iced coffee, no matter the weather but being pregnant I'm not sure if she's drinking coffee.

I'm about to sit down and contemplate what drink I'm going to get myself when she hobbles in the door. Her belly has definitely grown since I saw her a few weeks earlier. Spotting me, she slowly walks over, smiling from ear to ear.

I kiss her cheek, hugging her awkwardly, "Hey babe, you're glowing...hows Jai?"

She lets out a slight laugh, "He's a lot better...getting his cast off in about two weeks."

I pull out a chair for her to sit down, "That's good to hear. Are you still drinking iced coffee?"

"Yes, thank god, these babies haven't turned me off coffee."

I gape at her, she just said babies, not baby.

I obviously can't hide the shock from my face as she quickly says, "We um...had an ultrasound the other day."

"Yeah?"

"We're having twins, Austin," she beams excitedly.

"Oh my god, Anni that's amazing!"

"Yeah, we're so beyond excited."

"I bet and Bel being pregnant too, it's all happening for us," I reply with a hint of longing in my tone.

"Yeah, she'll be due soon, November I think."

I feign a smile, "I know...she hasn't spoken to me much though...I just wanna know if the kid is mine."

"I know Aust...but you'll be in the babies life either way," she says smiling at me as I start to walk up to the counter to order.

"Yeah..." I mutter, touching her arm when she's about to stand up to follow me, "I'm buying your coffee babe."

"Ok, thanks Aust," she replies smiling.

At the counter, I order her iced coffee and a Tim Tam chiller for myself. She's fidgeting in her seat and seems uncomfortable in my presence again when I sit back down.

Staring at me, she bites her lip, as though she's not sure what to say.

I laugh, the silence so awkward, "What do you want to say, babe? Cat got ya tongue?"

"Um," she laughs, "hows Dana?"

It's my turn to laugh, Anni is still so sweet and innocent.

"Good...I was actually thinking of asking her to move in with me...now Bella isn't home much."

Anni's whole face lights up, "Must be serious then. Are you in love with her?"

I can't meet her eyes when I reply, "I don't know Anni...I.."

Our drinks arrive and we both take an eager sip, letting the cool liquid quell the uncomfortable tension of our conversation.

"Just let your feelings guide you, Aust," she suggests, taking another sip of her iced coffee.

"Yeah...so are we good Anni?"

She puts her iced coffee on the table, chuckling softly, "Yeah Aust...I've missed you so much. I'm sorry for everything I said to you."

My heart pounds, and I can't help but smile when I reply, "Me too Anni....you know I'll always love you, yeah?"

"Yeah, I'll always love you too Aust...friends don't say goodbye."

"Yeah, especially best friends," I laugh, gulping down my chiller as fast as the straw will let me.

She stands up after taking a final sip of her iced coffee, "I need to head off, and take Jai home from physio."

I hug her, feeling as though I'm coming home.

"Ok, babe, text me yeah?"

She laughs lightheartedly, "Of course...um...Aust, will you come to our wedding?"

Her question makes me grin, "Of course babe...send me a text with the details, but I wouldn't miss it."

"Great," she beams, "I can't believe I'm going to be a pregnant bride."

"You'll look stunning no matter what, babe."

I smile at her.

She really looks beautiful pregnant, and I'm so overwhelmingly happy for her and Jairus.

"Thanks, Aust...bring Dana too. I can't believe you guys are together."

"Me too....we haven't even slept together yet but I just love being with her," I confess, biting down on my lip.

It's as though we've never been apart.

"That's great Aust...I kinda saw some sparks that day you came to Jai's game with me last year."

Laughing I ask, "Why didn't you say something?"

"I didn't want to interfere, and I didn't know what was going on with you and Bella."

"Fair enough...anyway I gotta get to boxing too. Don't be a stranger bestie," I jeer, poking the top of her belly gently.

"I won't Aust," she laughs, kissing me on the cheek as we head to the door.

Heading in opposite directions, we hug quickly and I call out to her, "Bye babe."

"Bye bestie," she coos, waving,walking away.

My heart swells with love for her, my best friend. How I've gotten through the last nine or so months without her in my life baffles me. I'm beyond glad that things have worked out. All I need now is to figure out my feelings for Dana, starting with actually kissing her properly like I wanted to weeks ago.

Fifty | Needing You Tonight

For an early November evening, it's absolutely freezing. I feel like an idiot cranking the fire but without it on I'm shivering even with trackies and a hoodie on.

I'm all set for a night in, beer in hand, the Switch docked and pizza box open on the coffee table, with a large supreme pizza ready to be devoured.

I'm about to lift a slice out of the box when the doorbell ding dongs again. I'm not expecting anyone else and I panic slightly, racing to the front door and skidding across the floor in my socks.

Opening the door I find Dana on the doorstep in tears.

"Hi Aust," she stutters through her tears.

I pull her inside, inviting her in by wrapping her in my arms. She's sobbing, her breath hitching as he tries to speak. Closing the door behind us, I take a step back to look at her and my heart breaks at how vulnerable she is.

She'd told me she was busy tonight catching up with some friends so her unexpectedly turning up on my doorstep in tears is concerning.

"Aww, gorgeous," I coo, pulling her close, picking her up bridal style and carrying her over to the couch where the fireplace is now blazing.

Putting her down gently I sit beside her and she leans into my chest, still sobbing when I ask, "What's wrong Dan?"

She looks up at me, wiping her tears away with her sleeve, "He..he came over tonight and he..." she mutters, cutting her words off with a wailing sob.

"What Dan? Who came over?"

"Ben....he's getting married to her."

"Who? Sara?"

"Yeah her, the bitch he had the baby with. Jai's ex."

"Why are you so upset about it Dan?"

"I don't know...I...I um.."

She's looking into my eyes like I have all the answers, but I've got no idea what to really say.

She hasn't told me much about her previous relationships, and since our awkward kiss at the footy, we've barely seen each other.

We'd facetimed, with her teasing me by stripping to her underwear one night, about to take off her knickers to touch herself when her roommate burst in.

It made my balls so blue, I'd considered calling Kaden but cheating isn't something I ever want to do.

Brushing a hand over Dana's cheek, wiping her tears away with my thumb, I muse softly, "He cheated on you gorgeous...he doesn't deserve you."

The look in her eyes is stabbing at my heart, I want to take the pain away so bad.

"He...um...he...I'm um...upset..." she stammers.

"Breathe Dan, I'm here gorgeous. Take your time."

She takes a deep breath in, exhaling, "I'm upset because he told me the only reason he cheated was because I couldn't give him everything."

Her confession confuses me, making me wonder for a moment what I've actually gotten myself into, getting with her.

"What do you mean Dan?"

She shifts back from me, sighing before she speaks, "I can't get pregnant Aust. When I was in high school I had such severe endometriosis that doctors had to remove both my fallopian tubes and my uterus is damaged as well, so even IVF is unlikely to work."

Tears sting her eyes again, and my heart is breaking for her when I pull her back closer to me again.

"Oh Dana I'm so sorry, but that's not a dealbreaker for everyone," I muse, kissing her forehead.

She sighs, letting out a raspy breath, "I've never told anyone else, other than Ben."

"Aww Dan," I reply wiping her tears away with my thumb again.

I don't know what else to say, I have no comforting words so instead, I press my lips to hers in a sweet kiss.

Her body melts against mine, our lips together in a searing kiss that she responds to at first when I lick her bottom lip but pulls back before I can take the kiss further.

Not able to meet my eyes, she speaks softly, "Austin, if you don't want me now I get it."

"Are you kidding Dan? I'm...I'm..."

She presses a finger to my lips, cutting my words off.

I sigh deeply, inwardly thanking her for cutting me off as I don't think I'm ready to confess my feelings.

Frankly, I'm not even sure what I feel.

She's gorgeous, turns me on with just a look, yet I don't think I have the words to verbalise that.

The last person to have that effect on me was Anni and seeing her a couple of weeks ago, that longing feeling had vanished.

I still love her but it's in that familiar way, that I'll always love her in some way.

Looking at Dana so vulnerable is breaking me apart.

I brush a stray hair from her cheek and she gazes up at me, muttering, "Me too Austin."

"Dan I want you...I know you're hurting but I wanna make you feel good."

She shifts uncomfortably, playing with the drawstring on her trackies and biting her lip.

My cock is aching, tenting in the front of my trackies.

All I want to do is pash her, feel her hands on me when I take her to bed.

"Aust I don't know....I..." she murmurs so sweetly, locking her eyes on mine.

Her irises darken with lust and I can't take it anymore, I want her, I need her now.

"Dana please could you be mine tonight?" I ask, my tone a tad seductive.

She looks at me for a moment, not saying a word.

My heart is hammering in my chest, awaiting her response that comes as a kiss against my lips, that takes the wind out of me.

It's a slow, sweet kiss and this time when I run my tongue along her lip, her tongue darts out to dance with mine.

Her fingers find my hair, gripping it her hands as she pulls me closer, moaning against my lips.

I bite her lip, moaning back, grabbing her by the waist to pull her onto my lap.

Breaking the kiss, completely breathless I brush the hair out of her face and she giggles.

"Mmm, Dana that was so much better than our first awkward kiss," I laugh, teasing her with a smirk.

She slaps my arm playfully, giggling, "Shut up, I was nervous."

"I know...so bedroom now?" I taunt, winking at her.

She smirks back, standing up and walking over to the fireplace.

Tapping her foot on the rug, she says meekly, "How about right here on the rug by the fireplace?"

A sweet blush rises up her cheeks as the words leave her mouth and I can't stop myself; standing up I practically trip over the edge of the rug, falling against her and grabbing her around the waist.

"Hey," she teases.

"Hey," I taunt back kissing her hard, before I break the kiss and respond to her question, "God Dana, that sounds so damn hot," I moan.

She grabs the front of my trackies, running her hand along my hard cock.

"Dan, gorgeous, fuck that feels good, but I really want your hands against my skin."

"Mmm," she moans so deliciously I swear my cock hardens more.

She lifts her jumper over her head, baring the skimpy Bonds bralette that barely hides her perfect mounds.

She slips a finger in the straps, teasingly edging them down her bare arms.

The fabric falls away from her breasts and she bites her lip as she pushes the bralette down her torso towards her stomach.

Bunching the fabric at her hips she pushes it and her trackies to the floor.

"Fuck, Dana, your body is so fucking breathtaking," I moan, kissing her again, cupping her arse, hidden beneath her cheeky knickers.

As we frantically kiss, our hands are all over each other. She makes quick work of dakking me, my trackies and boxers at the same time.

Our lips only break contact so I can lift my t-shirt off.

She runs fingers down the ridge in my abs, before gripping my hard cock in one hand and my balls in the other.

"Fuck me now, Austin, right here."

She sits down on the rug, taking my hand to pull me down, smashing a kiss to my lips. The fire is warm against my back, but the real warmth is coursing through my body, everywhere my skin touches Dana's is on fire.

Fifty-One | Dirty Fireside Fornication

Kissing Dana fiercely, I run my hands over her hips, making her buck them up against my aching cock.

The glow of the fireplace makes her lightly tanned skin glow, her cheeky pink Bonds knickers making her skin pop.

Flicking the elastic against her stomach I break the kiss, asking, "Gorgeous, can I take these off and taste you?"

Giggling she nods; I hook my fingers back in the elastic and pull them down her thighs, past her knees until she kicks them off at her ankles.

I take a moment to admire her naked before me.

She's not completely bare but has a small triangle of hair that literally points down to exactly where I want to put my mouth.

"Fuck Dana, your body is so fucking breathtaking."

She lets out a little whimper of pleasure when I plunge a finger inside her aroused core.

She's so wet, I moan feeling her arousal on my finger, playing with her clit.

Caz May

"Mmm Aust, fuck that's good."

"Really Dan?"

"Yes really," she mutters, biting down on her lip when I pull my finger out and lick it.

My eyes are locked on hers, and she pulls my finger to her lips, licking it and moaning.

"God damn it, Dana, that was fucking hot."

"Mmm, I want you to taste me Austin.;

I don't reply, instead spread her legs wide before I kneel in between them and run my tongue along her soaked slit up to her clit.

Teasing her, I bite the sensitive bud, lapping up all her sweet cream with my tongue.

Her arousal tastes beyond delicious, sweet but almost tangy.

Her moans as I give her an Aussie kiss are just as delicious and I know at that moment, her taste will be something I'll crave.

Stopping for a moment I look at her, smirking, "Dana you taste so fucking delicious gorgeous, but I want you to come with my cock buried in you."

Again she giggles, crawling back from me a little on the rug before she moves to be on all fours with her curvaceous arse in the air.

349

A devious smirk turns up at the corner of her lips, her gaze locked on mine when she taunts, "Fuck me doggy style, stud, hard."

I've never heard such dirty, hot and arousing words come from a naked chicks mouth.

My cock is aching, my mouth watering just at the thought of driving deep inside her wet core.

"God, gorgeous," I moan, kicking my boxers off my ankles.

She giggles, and hisses when I slap a hand against her bare arse.

"Mmm stud, that feels good," she groans, still looking back at me when I push my hard as steel cock inside her from behind.

Pulling in and out of her body, I revel in her delicious moans, loving the sound of my groin slapping against her arse.

"Fuck, Dana, god...it feels so fucking amazing to be inside you gorgeous."

"Mmm, I know," she moans, moving up so she's kneeling and her back is against my chest.

Tipping her head back to kiss me, I devour her mouth with our bodies still locked together.

She shifts her pelvis forward, ever so slightly, sweet torture for the moment I'm not inside her.

Emotions are rushing through my mind, her kiss against my lips and making her mine is beyond anything I've ever felt.

I've fucked many chicks doggy style, but something about the dirty fireside sex I'm sharing with Dana makes it feel like the first time.

"Dan, you're going to make me come so hard, gorgeous."

"Mmm, Aust, I'm going to come now. Kiss me please," she all but moans and begs at the same time.

Smashing my lips against hers again, I can feel her body twitching as I pound my throbbing cock inside her hard.

Biting on my lip, I feel her orgasm rock through her and wrap my arms around her body tightly.

My release as I pound into her hard again is sudden and overwhelming.

Breaking the kiss, she smirks at me, "Wow, fuck that was good Aust."

"Tell me about Dan, god...I...I." She cuts me off with a kiss, and I her squeeze my arms around her waist tighter when I break it.

"Stay the night please, gorgeous? I don't wanna let you go just yet."

"Um, yeah I'd love to," she replies softly crawling across the floor to grab her clothes.

I shake my head at her laughing, "I'm sleeping naked so you better be too, Dan."

"Ok, I guess," she smiles, suddenly all shy which makes my heart feel a little giddy.

Standing up I flick off the fire and grab Dana's hand to lead her down the hallway to my room.

I desperately want to fuck her again, slower and sweeter.

But at the same time, I just want to hold her naked in my arms.

I'm a fucking goner, I'm falling for her big time.

Fifty-Two | Waking Up Conjoined

Dana

A little dazed realising I'm naked and in a strange
bed, I freak out for a moment.
When I feel his arms squeeze me, pulling me closer I
roll over in Austin's arms to face him and his smile
warms my heart and makes my insides stir.

"Hey gorgeous, I didn't dream last night did I?"
I smile back, knowing my whole face glows with
memories of being together, first by the fireplace and
then again wrapped in his Spiderman doona, slow
and sweet, consuming sex.
"No Aust, you didn't."
He lets out a lighthearted laugh, kissing my forehead,
"Good, because it was beyond amazing and this...",
he gestures towards me in his arms, murmuring "is
the best way to wake up."
I can feel his morning wood pressing into my belly,
and his eyes are smiling at me.

I want to kiss him and get lost in the feel of his lips on mine again, but instead, I sigh, blurting out, "Aust, I'm scared."

He looks straight into my eyes with a concerned look, "About what Dan?"

"That you won't want me now we've slept together..." I blurt out again, biting on my lip.

He doesn't say anything, which makes panic rise in my chest, "I'm... I'm scared that you'll go back and get with Kaden."

He brushes a stray hair from my cheek, again sweetly kissing my forehead, "Oh Dana, that's not going to happen. I might be bi and enjoyed being with Kaden, but I'm here with you now and that's all I want."

"Really?" I ask tentatively.

"Yes, Dana, I'm falling for you," he declares, smiling wide.

My heart hammers, feeling as though it's about to burst out of my chest.

He hasn't exactly said 'I love you', but it's close enough. I want to tell him how I feel, having known I've been in love with him for months, "I...i..ll..." he cuts me off with a soft kiss, running his tongue along my lip before he pulls back before taking the kiss further.

"Don't Dan yeah?"

I shake my head, before kissing him harder and giving him the same teasing kiss.

"I could get used to this Austin."

He laughs, as though he's hiding hurt, "What? Being with me?"

"Nah, Yeah, waking up slow wrapped in your arms."

He sighs, "Oh right, then move in with me Dan?"

I gape at him, "Serious? Don't you need to ask Bella?"

"Why? She's never here much, now she's with Jax," he says with a serious tone, that sends my mind racing.

He sounds hurt about not seeing Bella, but then our night together was so incredible. I'm just so confused by how he's feeling.

He's saying one thing but implying something else with his tone.

"I don't know Aust...I can't leave my roommates in the lurch," I reply, making an excuse which is not at all how I feel and is nowhere near the truth.

"Ok, I get it," he says solemnly, frowning.

My heart sinks at the thought that I've hurt him.

"Aust I'm sorry...I didn't mean it like that...but not yet," I say, hoping he can sense the sincerity in my apology.

"Ok, but soon Dan, please...I don't want to let you go," he says in a tone that would make my knickers melt if I was wearing any.

"Me either Aust," I softly say before kissing him again.

He teases me by licking my lower lip, asking for entrance to lace our tongues together.

I give in, feeling desire building up, my clit throbbing with want. Every kiss, every touch we share is making me fall harder for him.

Continuing to kiss me, harder and more passionately, he moans against my lips, rolling over so he's on top of me. I can feel his hard cock pressing against my belly, and pulling back from the kiss I meekly tell him, "Aust, make love to me."

"Mmm Dana," he groans huskily, sliding inside my wet core as he smashes another kiss to my lips.

He rocks in and out, our bodies one and when he breaks the kiss, staring at me with longing in his eyes I feel a rush of warmth course through me.

"Dana, being inside you is so fucking incredible gorgeous."

Not replying I wrap my legs around his arse, pulling him deeper inside.

Wrapping my arms around his back, I pull him down for a lingering kiss that makes my heart pound.

He's right about the sex, every time it's amazing and I've never felt so connected to someone, never felt so in love.

Breaking the kiss, Austin moans, "Fuck Dan, I'm gonna come so hard, gorgeous."

His words send desire rushing through me, my climax building making my whole body tingle.

"Mmm, Austin," I moan, my words cut off when he pushes in deeper hitting that sweet spot that makes my peak hit me hard.

I bite down on my lip, trying to contain the scream of pleasure when I feel Austin loose himself inside me, moaning my name.

I scream out his name, drawing out the syllables on my tongue.

He's still inside me but not moving, completely satisfied when he presses his forehead against mine.

Against my lips, he whispers, "Dana, that was incredible, beautiful."

I laugh, pressing my lips against his lips softly before he rolls off and pulls me against his side.

My heart is pounding, partly because he has just called me beautiful instead of gorgeous and partly because I need to tell him how I feel.

Looking across at him, I smile, "Aust?"

He looks at me, his eyes locked on mine, "Yeah Dan?"

Again my heart is pounding, about to say the words to him, those three words I've not felt in such a long time, if ever.

I'd thought I'd loved Ben, but what I felt for him is nothing like what I feel when I'm with Austin.

That alone makes me sure of my next words to Austin.

"I love you," I say, pressing a kiss to his cheek.

I can feel his skin heat at the simple contact and when he kisses me back in response, I know, even though he doesn't say the words back that he's in love with me.

His kiss is sweet but possessive and loving.

I've never been happier.

I'm absolutely head over feet in love with Austin Belvinz and I'm pretty sure he's fallen just as hard as I have, even if he can't say the words back.

Epilogue | Everything's All Good

Christmas with my family is always a crazy affair and this year had been no different.

Things could have been awkward with Anni and Jairus over but with Dana by my side it felt beyond perfect like everything was all good in my world.

My whole family loved Dana, and she fit right in with my sisters, opening up to them.

Stepping into the kitchen, I find Mum washing the dishes from breakfast. When I pick up a tea towel, she smiles at me and says, "I'm glad you found someone now, baby boy. She's beautiful, Austin, outside as well as inside."

Drying a glass carefully, I smile when I reply, "Yeah mum she is... I'm..." I stumble on the last words, almost dropping the glass.

Mum lifts her hands from the soapy water after pulling the plug.

Gently drying her hands on the tea towel I'm still clutching she says, "What dear?"

I put it down, hugging her for a minute before I pull back.

"I'm in love with her Mum."

"I know Austin, that's clear. Have you told her yet?"

"No...but..."

She looks at me with that Mum knows best look, but also has a hint of chastising in her tone when she replies, "But what dear? She's clearly smitten with you."

"I know...she told me she loves me months ago...but I just haven't been able to get the words out."

"Is she the one Austin?" she asks in an odd tone that has me a little scared.

"Yes, Mum....she is," I declare puffing my chest out.

She smiles, "Then tell her how you feel... I've not seen you this happy in a long time especially with everything thats happened these past couple of years with Anni and Bella."

"Yeah, I know Mum...I love you...we better head off," I reply, hugging her again when Dana comes down the hallway from the bedroom dragging her bags behind her.

She stops in the kitchen, leaning against the bench. Mum pulls her into a hug, smoothing her hair down and kissing her forehead, "Lovely to meet you, dear," she coos with a wide smile on her face.

Dana smiles back, the elation all over her face, "You too, Mrs Belvinz. You have a lovely home and beautiful family."

It's so sweet, it makes my heart swell, and I kinda feel like an idiot for feeling so many emotions.

Lillie comes bounding into the kitchen just as I'm about to pick up our bags to head off.

She pulls me in for a tight hug, stretching up on her tiptoes to whisper in my ear, "Marry her Austy."

I laugh and whisper back, "Soon Lil, ok?"

Pulling back from the hug she nods and winks at me teasingly.

"Ready to go beautiful?" I ask Dana, grabbing her hand.

"Yeah, ready if you are stud," she says teasingly.

I can't help but laugh at the eager, happy smile on Mum's face.

Dad is in the lounge room as we head to the front door. He stands up, hugging Dana and I, patting me on the back in a well done my boy kinda way.

My family all gather at the front door, standing on the porch as Dana and I get in the car.

I toot the horn, waving as we drive off to head back to the city for a New Year's Eve that is going to be one to celebrate.

~~

As we drive back into the city a few hours later I head in the opposite direction to when we left just before Christmas.

Dana had moved in with me, taking Bella's bedroom, and I spent most nights since then a month ago wrapped in her overly pretty paisley pink doona, fucking her until she'd moan my name, until she'd repeatedly tell me she loved me.

I've wanted to say the words, every day, every time I look in her eyes, but they always catch on my tongue.

I feel them without a doubt, and seeing her with my family, as well as my convo with Mum cemented that in my head.

I'd pulled Anni aside on Christmas day, filling her in on my crazy little plan. She giggled like a kid in a candy store when I handed her the keys to our new place and told her to decorate it for my special surprise.

As I turn the ute down Glenferrie Road, Dana looks at me, shaking her head, "This isn't the way home, Austin."

"Yeah, it is," I laugh winking at her as I pull up to big black iron gates.

They open automatically and I drive in, across the white gravel driveway, to the parking area.

Dana's mouth is agape as she looks at the large white building in front of us.

It looks like a mansion but is about ten lavish apartments that I was shocked to find going so cheap for rent in Hawthorn.

It's surrounded by greenery and looks like something out of a kid's fairy tale.

Stopping the car, I'm about to cut the engine and explain, when Dana asks, "Austin who lives here?"

"We do Dan," I reply, laughing.

She looks at me incredulously, opening her mouth to protest but shutting it when I cut the engine and get out of the ute like I just sat on a bull ant's nest.

Going around to her side, I pull a makeshift blindfold out of my pocket, a long strip of black silk.

Opening her door, I extend my hand to help her out of the ute.

"Turn around gorgeous," I tell her, putting it over her eyes and tying it underneath her ponytail.

Softly I press a kiss to her lips, smirking at her even though she can't see me when she licks her lips after I break the kiss, "Aust what's going on?"

I laugh, "Just wait...trust me ok?"

She sighs and replies, "I trust you."

I grab her hand to lead her inside. She's apprehensive but follows me, squeezing my hand tightly.

After walking down the carpeted hallway reaching our new apartment I find the key under the mat where Anni had left it after she decorated it for me the night before.

Unlocking the door swiftly I lead Dana inside and close the door behind us. I take a moment to look around the room, at the rose petal covered lounge room, the banner across the window that says 'I love you' on it in fancy pink lettering.

It's so overly girly but so sweet and I know Dana will love it.

Kneeling down, taking the box from my back pocket I'm still holding her hand when I say, "You can take the blindfold off now, gorgeous."

Following my instruction, I smile wide, like the Cheshire cat when she looks down at me gaping. Opening the box I hold up the simple rose gold solitaire diamond ring to her. She giggles excitedly, covering her mouth with her hand.

Sighing deeply, exhaling a long breath I speak, "Dana Marie Ramera, since the moment we officially met, the day I bumped into you at uni, I've been slowly falling in love with you. I truly believe that we are meant to be and you're the reason I'm here, to love you and help you through anything. I honestly love you with all my heart, I'm yours, so will you marry me?"

She jumps and down on the spot, as I struggle to get to my feet, "Yes Austin, oh my god yes! Do you really love me?"

"Yes Dan, I really love you," I say through a laugh, standing up properly and slipping the ring on her finger, "I'm sorry it's taken me so long to tell you."

She laughs, pressing a kiss to my lips that tells me I'm forgiven for being a fool and taking so long to tell her how I feel about her.

"It was worth the wait, I love you too, Austin Maxmillan Belvinz."

Hearing her say my full name is beyond sweet music to my ears, "I'll never get tired of hearing you say that, gorgeous."

"Me either, so who helped set this up?" she says, looking around the room in wonderment.

"A sneaky best friend of mine," I laugh.

"Anni?"

"Yeah...I'm so glad she's back in my life. She was so excited when I asked for her help at Christmas."

Dana smiles at me, "It's funny how things work out right."

"Yeah, you said it gorgeous. Friends don't say goodbye."

"Neither do fiancee's," she laughs teasingly.

I laugh at her tease, "Well hopefully not. Care to celebrate our new place and engagement before we head to Anni and Jai's for new years?"

Her smile is seductive, "Sounds like a great idea....maybe we could find another use for the blindfold," she teases, running her fingers over the silk in her hand.

"I love the sound of that," I laugh taking her hand, admiring the ring on her finger as I lead her to the bedroom.

I've never been happier than I am at that moment. I'm about to make love to my beautiful fiancee, and can't wait for her to be mine forever.

Love is most certainly complicated, whether it's the love of a friend who doesn't say goodbye or a lover who crashes into your life to make you realise that feelings don't play fair.

They hit you like a freight train, and I've never been gladder to open my heart.

The commitment-phobe in me has finally faced my feelings. I might be in over my head, but without a doubt, I'm in love with Dana and everything's all good in my world.

The End

Australian Slang Glossary

Ute-Truck

Bludger- someone lazy, doesn't do much and possibly relies on social security benefits

Ripper- something really good/great

Ridgy-Didge- Cool

Bonzer-Great, awesome

Pash/ing/ed- to kiss/make out

Arvo- afternoon

Chunder- Vomit, throw up

Gobby- Blowjob

Aussie Kiss- going down on a girl

Daks- pants/trousers/underwear

Undies/Knickers/Jocks-underwear (female knickers, male Jocks, undies both)

Dakking- to pull someone daks down (see above)

Thongs- Footwear, otherwise known as flip flops

Esky- Cooler-you keep drinks cool in it

Dunny- toilet

Bogan-white trash/trailer trash

Old Fella- Your father/Dad

Franger- Condom, Trojan etc

Milo- a malt chocolate powered drink mix (can be made hot or cold)

Macca's-MacDonalds

Fair Dinkum- used to emphasise or seek confirmation of the genuineness or truth of something

Shark Week- A woman's monthly cycle

Stuffed if I know- *a nicer way to say fucked if I know*

That will barely cover your mappa Tassie- that will barely cover your vagina

AFL- Australian Rules Football

Playlists

Austin

https://open.spotify.com/user/cazcat25/playlist/

10WNI0ptdHBJFuWVhlG2Ti?si=wBQnTEn_S3WOFfuRsclD5g

Bella

https://open.spotify.com/user/cazcat25/playlist/

3bX5THFHuTeUmLJ1l61MoQ?si=kS7kEL8VT-2ykBRMv5nNpQ

Kaden

https://open.spotify.com/user/cazcat25/playlist/

2fhViTqNmotMp1abcsjaGY?si=RmAoJqPJTkuYD3WaZS-Ofg

Dana

https://open.spotify.com/user/cazcat25/playlist/
6rfGGG0yoCjiT59qLpP0wh?
si=sUv5uiWpQ4OiZkHQKIsK3Q

Annika, Jairus & Jaxon

https://open.spotify.com/user/cazcat25/playlist/
1meuXGFZtoHkTCdNs5w52T?
si=H3Z3J5CrRqSuo01O5wANHQ

About the Author

Caz May is a librarian/teacher by trade, but was always destined to be an author from a young age. In her spare time, she can be found devouring books or writing her own stories with characters that may not be the typical romance heroes but are loveable just as much.

Caz is married to her own real-life bearded hero and has two fur babies.

She lives for Iced coffee, especially from Gloria Jeans or a Farmers Union but pretty much just loves food in general.

When she's not writing, or reading a book most likely she can probably be found asleep or binge-watching shows on Netflix.

Check out her Instagram or other socials to get in touch.

Instagram- **@cazmay25**

Facebook- @CazMayAuthor

Wattpad- @Caz-May

Spotify- cazcat25

Website- https://cazcat25.wixsite.com/cazmay-author

Acknowledgments

Well, here we are! Acknowledgements for Book Two!

Firstly, I'd like to give a big shoutout to all of you who purchased Book One, straight away when I released it. You made my heart happy and I hope you also enjoyed Book Two just as much.

If I've met you on Wattpad or Instagram and you've been supporting me on this crazy journey, I thank you from the bottom of my heart.

There are too many of you to name, but if we've had a Direct Message chat or you've followed me and liked my content, I hope you know that your support is what keeps me writing!

I also want to give a wave from the pages to my sweet Nanna, who told me she wants a copy of Book one for her Eighty-Second birthday. I had to laugh, loving her support of my dreams but also knowing that Roommates Don't Kiss & Tell probably isn't her cup of tea. I wouldn't be her sweet innocent granddaughter anymore, but nevertheless her support is what matters most.

And again of course, I need to give a big shoutout and massive hug to my bearded hero again, my husband Cam.
This time around I've been a little calmer, and I think he's appreciated my less crazy self. He's always been a supporter of my dreams and a girl couldn't ask for a better partner in crime.

Anyway, that's all from me! For now!

Caz May

xx

Look out for Book Three

(Travis's Story)

Feelings

Don't

Play

Fair

Coming Soon

See below for a teaser

Prologue | Its all New

In Jai's penthouse at their New years eve party, I feel like a
fucking intruder, not able to feign happiness that another year has
slipped by without having accomplished anything near to what
my best friend has. Even though I've downed about five beers
and a couple of whiskeys, I'm a sad sack of shit, considering
flaking it way too early for New Year's Eve.

I'm listening to snippets of conversations around the room, trying
not to glance at Bella across the room.

She looks so carefree, her luscious brown hair in curls falling
around her shoulders that are exposed in a midriff baring tube top
that accentuates her tits into perfect mounds.

Dark denim high waisted shorts graze her belly button and
watching her I see the intake of breath when she laughs, tipping
her head back when Annika says something that I can't make out.
Gulping hard I clutch a hand to the fatty that's risen in the front of
my jeans, just fucking looking at her has me so turned on I want
to dak myself and wank in the middle of the crowded penthouse.

It hasn't even been a month since I'd woken up with her half naked in my bed. Not even a month since she rushed out of my house without another word and every fucking second she's been on my mind, especially when I'm so painfully hard thinking about her kisses that are a lightning bolt to my cock.

About to confront her, to smash my lips against hers and drag her back to my shitty apartment for the night, to rip the barely there clothes off her lightly tanned skin I'm sidelined by my best mate slapping an arm around my back.

He pulls me to his side in an awkward bro hug and I cringe a little when he slurs his words, "Travv...maate, youu nnneed a driiink."

"Nah, Jai man. I'm good, thinking of heading out. I...can't face her looking so fucking hot and not being able to have her."

He laughs, sobering up with his next words, "Haven't you already fucked her?"

It's my turn to laugh, but my chest constricts when I reply, "Man I wish. If I have and can't remember that's a fucking shame cause I want to fuck her until she can't walk."

"Well, get on it, " Jairus replies jovially and out of character. He'd always told me to stay away from Bella, even when we'd been partnered up in his wedding. But nothing could stop me from wanting the chestnut-haired beauty who is quite possibly the only chick who didn't succumb to my kicker melting charm. One look, one kiss from me usually got me a gobby, before I stripped a chick of clothes and tasted and fucked her until we came apart screaming like banshees.

In the past month, I've fantasised about what Bella would sound like when I make her come. I've thought about how beautiful she'd look when riding my cock, in my T-shirt the morning after. God, I fucking want her bad, more than I've wanted any chick in my thirty-two years of life; well since I was fifteen and I got my first hard on seeing the hot as hell P.E teacher changing after class one day. That was my wank goto thought for months, before I discovered actresses and the miracle that is porn.

But since meeting Bella a couple of years ago, even though we've barely spoken or touched until recently I've not needed to watch porn to wank. All I need to do was think of is her.

Jairus has left me standing in the middle of the room, and Annika is announcing something that I don't really care about until I saw Dana step up to hug her. She holds up her hand and Annika grins from ear to ear.

It makes sense when a guy steps up behind her, kissing her hair.

She's obviously engaged to him, Annika's best friend whose name I know also starts with 'a'.

My fuck buddy is gone now, and even though it turns my gut I saunter up to congratulate her before making a hasty exit to find a replacement bed buddy for the night.

I can't have Dana anymore, and I can't have Bella.I'm fucked and not in the cream my daks way.

Walking out of the apartment building, I pull my phone from my pocket to call a cab.

It's eleven thirty, practically the new year and I sigh deeply shoving my phone back into my pocket as I head to the tram instead, feeling defeated.

It's the worse New Year's Eve, ever.

I'm not getting a New Years kiss at midnight or fucking a girl into oblivion for the first day of January.

That is all new to me, and fuck it feels like shit.